"Anyway," he repeated, "now here we are..."

"Here we are," Livi echoed.

"And I thought maybe we should talk about...you know...where we go now."

He did meet her eyes then, and Livi responded with an acknowledging raise of her chin. But she didn't say anything because she had no idea where they should go now—especially factoring in that pregnancy test she had in that bag in the trunk of her cousin's car.

"How about we just put it behind us?" he suggested then. "Forget it happened. Start fresh..."

Easy for him to say.

"You want to help Greta," he went on, "and now she's kind of my job—her and the Tellers—so we'll be seeing each other. But Hawaii was...well..."

A one-night stand? A vacation fling? Pure stupidity on her part? Yes, what exactly should they call it?

As bad as the past two months had been for Livi, this was worse. This was excruciating. It felt like a brush-off. As if he was telling her that even though they'd slept together, he didn't want there to be anything more than that.

And while she certainly didn't, either, it was still a rejection. One she hadn't signed on for because she hadn't so much as entertained the idea of Hawaii going anywhere further.

THE CAMDENS OF COLORADO:
They've made a fortune in business.
Can they make it in the game of love?

Dear Reader,

After years of grieving the loss of her soul mate, Livi Camden has done something completely out of character. An attempt to escape the pain of a lonely wedding anniversary led to a night of abandon in the arms of a stranger. Filled with regret, now not only is she afraid she's pregnant, that man has suddenly come back into her life.

Software mogul Callan Tierney already has his hands full when he reconnects with the beauty he had to run out on. The former bad boy has lost his two best friends and inherited their nine-year-old daughter and her grandparents.

There couldn't be a worse time for Livi and Callan's paths to cross again, let alone for them to sort through what happened in Hawaii—the results of which Livi is keeping secret until she decides if Callan should be told at all.

Will she or won't she tell him? Can Callan handle any more? Those are questions that have to be answered amid the memories of their amazing night together. But it *was* an amazing night...

Hope you enjoy finding out what happens!

Happy Reading,

Victoria Pade

A Camden's
Baby Secret

———

Victoria Pade

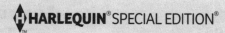

HARLEQUIN® SPECIAL EDITION®

Recycling programs
for this product may
not exist in your area.

ISBN-13: 978-0-373-65980-7

A Camden's Baby Secret

Copyright © 2016 by Victoria Pade

This edition published by arrangement with Harlequin Books S.A.

For questions and comments about the quality of this book, please contact us at CustomerService@Harlequin.com.

Printed in U.S.A.

www.Harlequin.com

Victoria Pade is a *USA TODAY* bestselling author. A native of Colorado, she's lived there her entire life. She studied art before discovering her real passion was for writing, and even after more than eighty books, she still loves it. When she isn't writing she's baking and worrying about how to work off the calories. She has better luck with the baking than with the calories. Readers can contact her on her Facebook page.

Visit the Author Profile page at Harlequin.com for more titles.

Chapter One

Maybe I shouldn't have come today, Livi Camden thought as she leaned against the wall in one of the downstairs bathrooms of her grandmother's house.

For over a week now she'd been having slight waves of nausea—mostly in the mornings. But on this warm, sunshine-filled Sunday afternoon—the second week of October—it became much worse than a slight wave the minute she'd come in and cooking smells had greeted her.

The bathroom had a window to the backyard and she opened it so she could breathe in the outside air.

Better...

The wave began to pass.

That was good. She hated feeling nauseous and she also didn't want to have to go home. She loved Sunday dinner at her grandmother's house with all her family—

even if she wasn't sure she was going to be able to eat much today.

Family had been everything to her since she'd lost her parents as a child and, along with her siblings and cousins, had become the responsibility of her grandmother. It was her family that kept Livi going when loss struck four years ago with Patrick's death.

Plus, GiGi had called and said she wanted a few minutes alone with her today, and whatever request her grandmother made of her, Livi did her best to fulfill—especially if it meant helping with the family project of making amends to those wronged by the Camdens in the past.

The discovery of her great-grandfather H. J. Camden's journals had confirmed all the ugly talk that had haunted the family for decades. It was rumored that the Camdens had regularly practiced underhanded and deceitful tactics to build their highly profitable empire of superstores.

The current Camdens were determined to do whatever they could to make up for the past. Quietly, so as not to invite false claims on them, they were finding ways to help or compensate those who had genuinely been harmed.

It was a cause Livi believed in and she was ready, willing and able to do her part.

Actually, she *hoped* that was why her grandmother wanted to talk to her.

Maybe doing something good and positive for someone else might make her feel better about herself these days. And it might also give her something to think about other than the biggest mistake she'd ever made in her life, for which she couldn't seem to stop chastising herself.

Another wave of nausea hit her and again she took

some deep breaths of cool backyard air, trying to relax. She was sure that stress over her horrible choice two months ago was causing the nausea.

"Hey, Liv, are you okay? You've been in there a long time."

It was her sister Lindie's voice coming from the other side of the door.

"I'm good. I'll be right out," she answered, glancing at herself in the mirror.

Her color was fine—her usually fair skin wasn't sallow, the blue eyes that people called "those Camden blue eyes" were clear and not dull the way they got when she was genuinely under the weather. She looked tired, but not ill.

So it probably *was* stress, she told herself. That's all. She was upset about what she'd done and that was making her stomach upset. When she calmed down and managed to put Hawaii behind her, her stomach would settle.

Leaving the bathroom, she tried not to breathe in too deeply the cooking smells as she went to the kitchen. But even shallow breaths caused the queasiness again. So she opened the door to the patio, angling a shoulder through the gap so she was once again breathing outdoor air without being completely outside.

Her sister and her cousin Jani were in the kitchen, gathering dishes, napkins and silverware. They both paused to watch her.

"Are you still sick with that weird flu?" Lindie asked her.

A touch of the flu—that was the excuse she'd given the first few days that she'd been late getting to work while she'd waited out the nausea at home.

"It can't be the flu—that doesn't last as long as this has," Jani contributed.

The downside of being so close to her family—they sometimes knew too much.

"Okay, so it's not the flu," Lindie said. "But what is it? You've been all wound up ever since you got back from Hawaii."

"Travel can make a mess of my stomach," Livi hedged.

"But you've been back for weeks—plenty of time for your stomach to readjust."

"Her wedding anniversary was while she was there," Lindie pointed out to their cousin, as if she'd just hit on a clue. Then to Livi she said, "Was it bad this year? Did it set off something and put you back in a funk, stressing you out?"

Oh, the anniversary set off something, all right, Livi thought. But she couldn't say *that*.

"My anniversary is never a good day." And this year her response had been completely over-the-top and stupid. But again, she couldn't tell anyone, so instead she said, "I don't know. Maybe I've been a little tense since then. And that always gets to my stomach. I'm sure it'll pass, the way it always does," she added with confidence.

But those smells were getting to her again, so she opened the door a little farther and moved a few more inches over the threshold.

Her left hand hung on to the edge of the door. Her left *ringless* hand.

And just the way Lindie had before Livi went into the bathroom, Jani noticed.

"Am I seeing what I'm seeing?" she exclaimed. "You took off your wedding rings? That's probably it!"

"Oh, sure, I should have thought of that," Lindie concurred.

"Did you decide in Hawaii?" Jani asked. "That's a big deal, taking off your rings. No wonder you're all tied up in knots! Was it the anniversary that finally got you there? That *had* to be agonizing for you. And now you've done it… But that's good," her cousin added quickly. "That's great! Of course, it couldn't have been easy for you, and it's bothering you and causing the tummy trouble. But don't put them back on! This is the first step for you to really heal."

Livi felt like such a fraud. Along with the intermittent nausea, for some reason her fingers had swollen and she *couldn't* get her rings on. She had every intention of wearing them again when the swelling went down.

But since this assumption provided such a ready excuse to appease her sister and cousin, she let them think what they wanted.

Which might not have been the best course, because then Lindie said, "Maybe when she feels better we can even get her to go on a date."

"No," Livi interjected firmly, thinking that she couldn't let this go too far.

"You *need* to, Livi," her cousin added. "Usually people have their first love, get their heart broken—"

"Or break someone else's heart," Lindie interjected.

"Then do a lot of testing the waters with other people before they find Mr. Right," Jani finished. "But you—"

"Married my first love."

"And missed getting the experience of casual dating. And now you're just stuck in this limbo—Patrick is gone and you don't know how to do what the rest of us learned a long time ago. You need to get comfortable with the whole dating thing. Then maybe you'll be able to—"

Don't say move on again! Livi wanted to shout.

Instead she said, for what felt like the millionth time, "Patrick wasn't just my first love, he was also my *only* love, and you guys need to accept that. I have."

"People can have more than one love in a lifetime, Livi," Lindie persisted. "Look at GiGi—she has Jonah now."

"And I'm happy for her," Livi said. "But Patrick was *it* for me."

"So maybe you won't find another love-of-your-life," Jani reasoned. "Maybe you'll just find a close second. But that's still something. Don't you want companionship at least? Someone to have dinner with? Someone to go to the movies with? Someone to—"

"Have sex with?" Lindie said bluntly.

Oh, that made her *really* queasy!

"No," Livi said forcefully, meaning it. And unwilling to tell either her sister or her cousin just how clearly she now knew it was a mistake to veer off the course she'd set for herself since Patrick.

"I'm fine," she went on. "Honestly. I'm happy. I'm content. Sure, I wish things had turned out differently and Patrick and I had gotten to grow old together. But that wasn't in the cards and I've accepted it."

"What about kids?" Jani asked, resting a hand on her pregnant belly, round and solid now that she was entering her third trimester.

Livi shook her head. "I get to have all the fun with my nieces and nephews—more of them coming all the time these days—and none of the work. I'll spoil every one of them and be their favorite aunt and they'll like me better than their mean parents who have to discipline them. Then, when I'm old and gray in the nursing home, they'll all come to visit me just the way they do you guys."

Jani rolled her eyes. "It won't be the same."

"It'll be close enough."

"Close enough to what?" Georgianna Camden—the matriarch of the Camden family—asked as she came into the kitchen.

"Livi thinks that being an aunt is better than having kids of her own," Lindie answered.

The seventy-five-year-old grandmother they all called GiGi raised her chin in understanding but didn't comment.

"She took off her wedding rings, though," Jani said, her tone full of optimism.

"Oh, honey, I know how hard that is," GiGi commiserated. "Good for you!"

"Her stomach is bothering her because of it," Lindie explained.

"Well, sure. I'll make you dry toast for dinner—that always helps. But still, good for you," the elderly woman repeated like a cheering squad.

Livi was feeling guiltier by the minute. When this whole queasiness-swollen-fingers thing passed and she put her rings back on, she knew everyone would worry about her all over again.

But there was no way she could explain what was really going on. The true reason for her queasiness—the fact that she was so upset over what had happened in Hawaii—had to be her secret.

So she changed the subject and said to her grandmother, "I could use something to take my mind off everything, GiGi. I was hoping you wanted to talk to me today to tell me you have one of our projects for me."

"As a matter of fact, that *is* why I wanted to talk to you," she said, her tone more solemn. "Why don't we go sit outside and talk?"

Thinking that that was a fabulous idea, Livi wasted no time slipping out onto the back patio. Luckily, the beautiful Indian summer that Denver was enjoying made the weather warm yet.

Livi went as far from the house as she could to escape the cooking odors, and sat on the brick bench seat beside the outdoor kitchen they used for barbecues.

GiGi followed her, pulling one of the chairs away from a glass table nearby to sit and face her.

"This one makes *me* sick," her grandmother announced as a prelude. She then told the story of the Camden sons and Randall Walcott, who had been Howard and Mitchum Camden's best friend and so close to the entire family that GiGi herself—Howard and Mitchum's mother—had known him well.

As Livi listened her stomach finally did settle, allowing her to concentrate on what GiGi was telling her.

"Which brings us to today," GiGi said, when she'd given her the background. "I only read about what your grandfather and H.J. and my sons did a few weeks ago. I've been looking into it ever since to see how we could make some kind of restitution—I thought it would be to Randall's daughter. She and her husband and little girl live in Northbridge..."

"So you called Seth," Livi guessed. It was a reasonable conclusion given that her cousin and his family lived in the small Montana town on the family ranch, overseeing the Camden agriculture interests.

"I did," GiGi confirmed. "And he told me that two months ago, Randall's daughter and her husband were killed in a car accident. Thankfully, their little girl, Greta, wasn't with them."

"How old is she?" Livi's voice was full of the sympathy she felt, because she could identify with the childhood loss of parents.

"She's only nine."

"And does she have a GiGi?" Livi asked. It was her grandmother who had been the salvation of her and her siblings and cousins when their parents and grandfather had all died in that plane crash. If anyone had to suffer through what they all had, the best thing that could happen to them was to have a grandmother like they had.

"She only has the Tellers—the grandparents on the husband's side. But Seth said that Maeve Teller has health issues of some kind and apparently neither Maeve or her husband, John, are in a position to raise the little girl. There's some situation with a family friend who was granted guardianship of her in the parents' will. A single man—"

"They left a little girl with a single man? How is he handling that? Does Seth know him?"

"Seth wasn't able to get a name, though he heard that there's something about him that doesn't sit well with folks around there for some reason. But the parents must have trusted whoever this man is or they wouldn't have left him their child."

Livi hoped that was true.

"At any rate," GiGi went on, "I don't know what the financial situation is. The Tellers only have a small farm and Seth says it isn't doing well, so he doubts there's much money there, especially if Maeve has medical bills.

And regardless, the little girl can't be inheriting anything like what she would have if we'd treated her grandfather fairly."

"That's the ugly truth," Livi agreed.

"So what I want you to do is go to Northbridge and make sure this child has the care she needs now and anything she might need in the future. Let's make sure that whoever this family friend is wants her…"

"Hopefully, finding himself guardian of a nine-year-old girl didn't come as an unpleasant surprise," Livi muttered.

"Hopefully," GiGi agreed. "But let's make sure that he's capable of taking care of her, that he'll give her a good home. And maybe we can set up a trust fund for her, money for her college, whatever it takes to make sure she has the kind of life she would have had if…" GiGi's voice trailed off as if she was too disgusted, too disappointed, too ashamed of what her own husband and sons had done to repeat it.

"So I'll sort of be her GiGi," Livi said affectionately, not wanting her grandmother to go on feeling bad.

She was pleased when GiGi smiled in response. "Not necessarily a GiGi, but maybe the little girl could use a sort of big sister or a mentor—a woman in her life, too, even if everything is going well with the guardian. Or maybe she won't need anything but to be provided for financially. However, we won't know that until you check things out."

Livi nodded.

"Are you well enough?" the gray-haired woman asked.

"I'm fine. I feel better when I have a lot to do and don't think about…things. Like I said, I need a distraction."

"If you get tempted to put the rings back on, maybe

consider wearing them on your right hand. I still do that sometimes."

"I know," Livi said, fighting another surge of guilt at what she'd allowed her family to believe.

Once more wanting to skirt around it, she went back to what they'd been talking about. "I have some things I have to take care of this week that can't be put off. How about I go to Northbridge next Saturday and look up Greta and her grandparents and this guardian on Sunday?"

"The sooner the better, but I suppose another week won't make any difference," GiGi said. Then she stood. "Now let's go get you some dry toast for that stomach of yours."

Livi dreaded going back into the house and the smells that brought on the queasiness, so she said, "I'll be right there. I just want to sit here a minute."

And think about how nice it would be if her stomach stayed as settled as it was right then.

If her fingers returned to their normal size.

And if her period would start this month even though it never had last month.

Because if only it would, then she really could forget all about Hawaii.

And the man who had—for just one night—made her forget too many other things...

Chapter Two

"We knew there was some bad blood between Mandy's father and your family from a long time ago, but she never talked about it and, well…"

"Considering the way her father went out we never brought up anything about him, so all we know is that there *was* bad blood."

What sweet Maeve Teller had tried to say diplomatically, her blunt husband, John Sr., finished.

Livi had arrived in Montana on Saturday evening, to discover Seth had taken his wife and new baby to visit Lacey's father in Texas. He'd left the keys to his cars and trucks for Livi to use—as well as the directions to the Teller farm—and promised to be back Sunday night. Tonight.

Livi had actually been glad to have the Northbridge house to herself for a while. Along with the continuing bouts of nausea and the swollen fingers, she was so easily tired out these days that she'd been happy to go straight to bed.

Unsure what kind of reception she might receive, and not wanting to risk an outright refusal to be seen, she'd arrived at the Tellers' farm without warning at two o'clock. The door had been opened by a woman who looked to be her own age—Maeve's nurse. She hadn't even asked who Livi was. She'd merely said hi, and when Livi told her that she was there to see the Tellers, the woman had invited her in without any questions.

Small-town warmth and friendliness—it had made it easy for Livi to get to the living room, where an elderly couple was playing a board game with a little girl.

Livi had introduced herself and offered the condolences of the entire Camden family for the loss of Mandy and John Teller Jr. The Tellers had asked how her grandmother was—GiGi was a well-known native of Northbridge— and after briefly updating them about her, Livi had explained that Randall had grown up as the best friend of Livi's father and uncle, and that GiGi had thought of Randall as her third son. That having just heard about the accident that had cost Randall's daughter her life and orphaned his granddaughter, GiGi had requested that Livi make this visit on her behalf.

Though the Tellers admitted that they knew there was more to the story—that there had been, eventually, a very bitter parting of the ways between Randall and the Camdens—Livi's sympathies had been accepted with grace. What followed was an hour with the Tellers and Greta. And also with the home health care nurse, Kinsey Madison, who was looking after Maeve, who had broken her arm, shoulder and leg in a fall, leaving her in plaster casts and a wheelchair.

Livi learned that Maeve and John Sr. were both eighty years old. And while John Sr. didn't have any disabilities that Livi could discern, she'd seen enough to know that he moved slowly and very stiffly, barely lifting his feet. So even he was nowhere near as agile as seventy-five-year-old GiGi or her seventy-six-year-old new groom, Jonah. In fact, the attentive nurse seemed to be subtly caring for John Sr. almost as much as she was caring for Maeve, so Livi understood why Greta's parents had not left her guardianship to the elderly couple.

Livi didn't have any difficulty establishing rapport with the Tellers or with Greta, all of whom she liked instantly. And the more they all visited, the more Livi saw how much the Tellers doted on the little girl. They obviously loved her dearly.

For her part, Greta—an outgoing nine-year-old with long blond hair and big brown eyes—had quickly warmed to Livi and was clearly dazzled by her fashionable clothes and hairstyle. She was so enthralled that Livi had removed the scarf she'd used as a headband today and gifted it to Greta, who was now sitting on the floor at her feet so Livi could tie it around the girl's wavy locks the way she'd been wearing it herself.

Even while she was pampering Greta, Livi went on chatting with Maeve and Kinsey. John Sr. wasn't particularly talkative, but threw in a few comments from time to time.

All in all, Livi thought it was going smoothly, that she'd lucked out, that this particular restitution would be easily accomplished.

"You look beautiful, Greta," Kinsey declared when

Livi was finished and the nine-year-old looked to the nurse for approval.

"I wanna see," Greta announced, running from the room and bounding up the stairs to the second level of the old farmhouse, presumably to a mirror.

With the child out of earshot, it seemed like an opportunity for Livi to say, "I'm not sure what Greta's needs are, but we want to do whatever we can for her now and from here on."

"And you would be?" a deep male voice interrupted, coming from behind Livi.

Maeve and John Sr. were sitting across from Livi and they both looked beyond her to the man who had just come in.

Livi noted that John Sr. instantly scowled, while Maeve smiled and said, "This is Ms. Camden—"

"Oh, no, I'm just Livi."

"Camden," the man behind her repeated scornfully at the same time.

Undeterred, Maeve smiled at her and said, "Livi," to confirm that she would use her first name. Then she added, "Callan is an old friend of Mandy and John Jr.'s. He's Greta's godfather and now her guardian."

Livi froze.

Callan?

It wasn't a common name.

And it was the name of the man she'd spent the night with in Hawaii. The man she'd exchanged only first names with.

The man who had run out on her.

But it had to be a coincidence.

It *had* to be...

Then he came around into her line of vision.

And everything in her clenched into one big knot.

It was the same name because it was the same man.

Livi didn't know whether to slap his face or crawl away in shame.

"Livi?" he said when he got a look at her face, his voice full of shock. His expression almost instantly showed embarrassment before confusion sounded, too, as he said, "You're a *Camden*?"

"You two know each other?" John Sr. asked.

Neither of them answered immediately.

Then Callan said, "We've met."

"Once," Livi added, her gaze locked with his.

Actually, they knew hardly anything about each other. They'd talked about why they were in Hawaii—her for a sales convention, him for a business meeting. Beyond that?

They'd talked about the enormous sea turtle on the beach right in front of where Livi was sitting when he'd joined her without an invitation. About the weather. The hotel. The restaurants and food. The sites. About how beautiful the sunset they were watching together was.

But they hadn't talked about anything of any importance.

And she'd had a completely different impression of him—as the businessman she'd assumed he was. Right now, he looked more like a cowboy, in faded blue jeans and a soiled chambray shirt that still managed to accentuate his broad, broad shoulders.

The hair was the same, though—thick auburn, short on the sides and slightly longer on top, where it was carelessly mussed. Also the same was the model-handsome face, lean and sculpted, with a strong jaw shadowed with stubble around thin but hellishly sexy lips. His slightly longish nose was straight and narrow. His penetrating eyes as dark as black coffee, beneath brooding brows and a square forehead.

And tall—he was so tall. And muscular.

Nothing at all like her Patrick.

Which had been part of the reason for that night...

Livi swallowed with some difficulty, trying to manage so many emotions at once—the shame and humiliation, but also the attraction she wished she could repress. Because she couldn't help appreciating what an impressive, imposing specimen of a man he was.

"I didn't know you were a cowboy from Montana," she said weakly.

"Cowboy?" John Sr. commented, breaking through Livi's shock. "He isn't really that."

"He is when he's getting his hands dirty doing our work around here," Maeve retorted. "And, yes, Livi is a Camden," the older woman confirmed to Callan. "She's Seth Camden's cousin, Georgianna Camden's granddaughter, and she came to offer sympathies and help with Greta."

Livi watched Callan's thick eyebrows dip together in a frown. "Help with Greta," he repeated without inflection. But the frown was enough to let her know that he wasn't as receptive to the idea as the Tellers had already seemed to be. "Why would a Camden want to do that?"

Suspicion. It was clear as day in his voice then.

So much for this going smoothly...

And despite what had happened in Hawaii and how monumental it was to her, Livi realized that their personal history was now on the back burner for him. That they'd veered into anti-Camden territory. John Sr. and Maeve hadn't seemed to know the details of the bad blood between the Camdens and Randall Walcott, but Livi was willing to bet Callan knew the whole story—and held a grudge.

"I know that once upon a time there was a falling out with the Camdens and Randall Walcott—"

"A *falling out*?" Callan repeated with an unpleasant huff. "You people played that guy for a sucker. You lured him in and then pulled the rug out from under him."

Livi took a deep breath, wishing she could deny any part of what he'd just laid at her family's doorstep, but knowing she couldn't. The harsh, often unethical behavior of the senior Camdens was the very reason she and her siblings and cousins were working so hard to make restitution.

"Until very recently none of the Camdens who are around today—me, my brothers and sister, my cousins and our grandmother—knew what went on all that time ago," she said. "My grandmother knew Randall Walcott as a boy her sons grew up with, worked with—"

"They *worked* him, all right," Callan continued with a sneer. "They had their old man give him advice on how to start his shoe business. Even gave him a loan so he could expand it. But about the time he had everything up and running they called in the loan, knowing he couldn't pay. Then they took over his company, stealing what he'd started and built up. You people still sell Walcott Shoes, if I'm not mistaken."

"You people" again...

"I was only two years old when it went down," Livi felt compelled to point out. "And no one alive today had anything to do with it. None of us would let something like that go on now and—"

But Callan seemed determined that the entire story be

told, because he interrupted her to go on. "Mandy's dad ended up with nothing! That poor bastard had to come here with his tail between his legs and move his family in with his in-laws. Mandy told me all about it. She was just a kid, but when you see your dad as upset and beaten down as he was, you remember it. She hated what had happened to him…especially with what happened next, when after two years of more failure here he ended up putting a gun to his own head—"

"Shh, shh, shh…" Maeve whispered suddenly, apparently spotting Greta just before she returned to the room, having changed clothes.

"I wanted to put on my dress that goes with the scarf," the little girl announced. Then, spotting Callan, she laid a small hand to the hair adornment and said, "Look, Uncle Callan—Livi gave me this and tied it like she had it. Isn't it pretty?"

"It is," he confirmed, but his voice was tight.

"Come on, Greta," Kinsey said in a hurry, as if she was looking for any reason to escape this scene herself. "Let's go see how many other things will match the scarf."

The nurse held out her hand to the little girl and Greta took it eagerly, chattering as if Kinsey was a girlfriend as they both left the room.

Not until they heard a door closing upstairs did anyone speak.

Then Callan broke the silence. "Any Camden is the last person on earth Mandy would want near her kid," he said flatly, as if that put an end to the discussion.

"But this girl didn't have nothin' to do with anything that happened all those years ago," John Sr. argued. "It's nothin' to do with Greta, neither, and far as I can see, it's nothin' to do with you no way, Tierney—"

His last name is Tierney?

The name meant nothing to Livi, but she tucked it away as information she might need.

"Least you could do," the elderly man went on, "is hear out Livi here. We hardly know Seth Camden, her—" he looked to Livi "—cousin, is it?"

"Yes," she said.

"We don't barely know him, but when word got around town about our troubles, he sent his crew over here to help out. Come pickin' time, they did our whole harvest. And when I asked what we owed them they said that they were on the Camden clock, that Seth Camden was just bein' neighborly and wantin' to help us out, and not to even mention it. Seems to me that's a sign of what this young lady is sayin'—the new breed isn't like the old one."

Livi took that endorsement as her cue. "We want to make up for what was done all those years ago. Greta is Randall Walcott's only living descendent and the only person we can compensate. We want to make sure she's looked after and has anything she needs. *Anything*—care and attention, a trust fund. A college fund, maybe—"

"She doesn't need your money," Callan said, as if financial matters were of no importance.

"But we want to take care of whatever she *does* need," Livi persisted.

Just then Greta came bounding back into the living room, running straight to Livi. "Look at this other scarf I found!"

"That's the sash to your Christmas dress, sweetheart," Maeve said.

"But it's *like* a scarf!" Greta insisted to her grand-mother, before honing in on Livi again. "Can you teach me how to tie it like you did? And could you paint my fin-gernails like yours, too? I think that would look nice with my outfit. Oh! You have pierced ears!" she exclaimed, apparently just noticing. "My mom's ears were pierced and she said I could have mine done, too. My friend Raina's mom pierced hers—can you do that?" the little girl asked eagerly.

"Greta, where did you go?" the nurse called from up-stairs. "Come back and see—I found something we can tie in your doll's hair like you wanted."

"I'll be right back!" Greta promised Livi, before charging out of the room again.

As she did, Maeve said, "She's attached to Kinsey. Follows her like a shadow. But what will happen when I'm better and don't need a nurse anymore? Then an old lady will be the only woman Greta has paying any kind of close attention to her. What she needs is a younger one, somebody who can give her what Mandy would have. And she seems to have taken to you, Livi…"

GiGi had suggested something similar—that Greta would need a woman in her life. And that had been some-thing Livi had thought she might be able to do, even if it was long distance. She could make frequent trips to Northbridge, she'd decided. And maybe Greta could oc-casionally come to Denver on long weekends or vacations from school, to give her guardian a break.

Only, now that Livi knew *who* Greta's guardian was, she couldn't say she was eager for any contact that might put her in the position she was in right now.

So she said, "I'd be happy to spend time with her, to act as a big sister. But I live in Denver. Seth might know of a woman here—between the two of us I'm sure we could find someone for her."

"Denver is where we're all headin'," John Sr. said under his breath, not sounding happy about it.

"That's where Callan lives," Maeve explained. "And he wants to look after us now that our John Jr. can't. We aren't doing so well on our own anymore."

Then I don't have an out? Livi was near panic at the idea of having to face Callan on a regular basis.

"I don't know about having her around Greta," Callan said, sounding frustrated at having his stance ignored. "She's come at us out of the blue. How do we know she doesn't have something up her sleeve, the way her family did with Greta's grandfather?"

"It isn't like you don't have some things to answer for in your own past," John Sr. grumbled to Callan. "And that was all you, not some long-gone relatives. Didn't keep Mandy and our John from lettin' you be around Greta."

Callan looked thunderous, which Maeve must have noticed, because she rushed to speak next. "I have good instincts about people and Livi seems like a nice person who's just wanting to make things right. Everybody makes mistakes. It's what they do to correct them that matters."

There was an underlying message in that, aimed at both John Sr. and Callan, but Livi had no idea what that message was. It kept both men quiet, though, while Maeve seemed to take the reins.

"I think it could be really good for Greta to have you be her big sister, Livi," the elderly lady said then. "To have a young woman's guidance so I don't have to worry that I'm not up-to-date enough for her. Today, meeting you, is the happiest I've seen her since we lost her momma and daddy. So if you're willing to take that little girl under your wing to atone for the past, I think we'd be lucky to have you."

It appeared that both men knew better than to argue with her.

But with resignation in his almost-black eyes, Callan said to Livi, "Greta is my responsibility now and I'll be watching to make sure you're on the up-and-up with this."

He'd be *watching*? Did that mean that he was going to make sure he was around whenever she was with Greta?

Oh, great, that's all I need.

But what could Livi say? That he was the glaring reminder of her worst mistake and she didn't want to face him over and over again?

GiGi had given her the task of performing restitution to Greta. It was her job to make sure Greta was well taken care of, that the little girl's needs were met—no matter what. Livi had to see it through. She didn't have a choice.

Maybe this is my punishment for Hawaii, she thought.

But without any way to back out now, she took a deep, bracing breath, plastered a smile on her face and said, "We just want to do something for Greta's good."

Regardless how difficult it might prove to be for Livi.

Because despite the way this had started out today, she was now afraid it was going to be very, very difficult...

"I'll go in and say hello to John, pay him directly."

"Yeah, sure," Callan said to the man whose truck he'd just loaded with hay bales.

There had been an edge of distrust in Gordon Bassett's voice, but Callan ignored it. Disdain and distrust for him in Northbridge was an old song Callan knew well. And apparently that was never going to change. It was the price he paid for being the kid from the other side of the tracks. A kid who had earned the reputation as a troublemaker.

But Callan had too many other things to think about at the moment to care about that. Actually, he wasn't even looking at the man he'd known all his life. He was watching the woman he now knew as Livi *Camden* drive away. And wondering what the hell was going on lately. Life was throwing him one curve ball after another.

Beginning in the middle of the night he'd spent with her.

If she'd told him her last name when they'd met at that beach bar in Hawaii, he might have left her sitting alone to watch the sea turtles and the sunset by herself.

Oh, who was he kidding? Even knowing what kind of people she came from, he probably would have stuck around.

She'd been too damn gorgeous sitting there in the fading sunlight with her long, bittersweet-chocolate-colored hair draping over her sexy bare shoulders. When she'd looked up at him with eyes that were a darker and more beautiful cobalt blue than the clear sky in the distance, eyes set in the face of an angel, he wouldn't have pulled away no matter what. Not with the mood he'd been in, having just accomplished a buyout he'd been working on for a year. He'd wanted to kick back and celebrate a little at day's end—so yeah, he'd have probably stuck around even if he had known she was a Camden.

He just wouldn't have ever told Mandy about it.

But the Livi of Hawaii *was* a Camden.

And now their paths had crossed again.

Two curve balls for the price of one...

He watched Livi's car get farther and farther away. He'd had every intention of going out to that car with her when she left so he could talk to her alone about Hawaii.

But then Bassett had showed up for his hay and Callan had had no choice but to head out to load the truck.

Now she was gone and he felt like an even bigger heel than he'd felt in the last two months whenever the thought of Hawaii came to mind.

As big a heel as she no doubt thought he was.

Not that they'd made any plans. Any promises. It had even been Livi who had dodged talk of what she'd called their "real lives."

But still, to take off without a word, without even thinking about her...

To be honest, in that moment he hadn't been thinking about anything but that middle-of-the-night phone call.

That lousy, freaking call that had caused his phone to vibrate enough to wake him without waking Livi, so he could take it into the living room of his suite and not disturb her.

That lousy, freaking call that had literally knocked the breath out of him, leaving him dazed and operating on autopilot, struggling to deal with the news that his two closest friends—Mandy and John Jr.—had been involved in a horrible car accident. That J.J. was barely holding on to life. That Mandy was already dead.

Callan had thrown on the clothes Livi had helped him discard hours before. Once he was dressed—taking nothing with him other than his wallet and cell phone—he'd rushed out of that suite, calling his pilot to arrange an emergency flight for his private jet, to get him to Montana immediately.

Calling the concierge to explain the situation and get the man to see to packing his bags, checking him out and sending the bags to him later.

Calling his assistant to get to Montana ahead of him and begin dealing with the nightmare.

By the time Callan was on his way to the airport, and finally remembered the woman he'd left in his bed, it was already too late.

He'd called his hotel room from the plane—no answer. He'd talked again to the concierge, who had gone to the suite while he was still on the line.

But Livi was gone, and there was no way for Callan to contact her when all he knew was her first name.

They'd gone from the beach to his suite, so he had no idea what room had been hers, no way of trying to get a belated message to her. No way of ever letting her know what had happened, and that he'd hoped and expected their time together to end much differently.

At the very least, it wouldn't have ended with him disappearing into thin air.

He felt rotten for how he'd treated Livi, even if he did have a reason for it. Under other circumstances, if they'd met again, he would have apologized, explained, maybe tried to make it up to her somehow.

But under these circumstances?

Nothing about these circumstances was normal.

She *was* a Camden. He knew how Mandy had felt about the Camdens—any generation of them. She would never have trusted them. And she would never have let any one of them near Greta.

And why *had* Livi come around?

Callan couldn't say that he trusted a Camden's motives, either. Not after what he knew they'd done to Mandy's dad.

Did Livi Camden have something up her sleeve?

She was the first Camden to make any contact since they'd got what they wanted all those years ago. It was something Mandy had always added when she'd told the story—that they'd never so much as said they were sorry, not even when her dad died...

And that was what they did to supposed *friends*.

Now Callan was being pressured to let one of them near Greta?

But just how hard-line could he be with her, after the way he'd abandoned her in Hawaii, even if there had been a good reason? Not to mention just how hard-line could he be going up against the Tellers, who had taken an instant liking to Livi and seemed willing and eager to have her mentor their granddaughter?

The Tellers, who he owed.

The Tellers, who he'd promised John Jr. on his deathbed he would take care of.

That promise was already hard enough to keep, given the way John Sr. refused to trust him. If Callan went against the man in this, it would just make the tensions between them that much worse.

It didn't seem like this was where to draw a line at all, except for Mandy's feelings about the Camdens...

Could he really let Livi into her daughter's life?

It felt wrong.

But apparently only to him.

By now, Livi Camden's car was out of sight. And with the weight of everything bearing down on him, Callan bent over, hands to knees, and stared at the dirt under his feet.

He'd had one hell of a lot to figure out even before he'd walked into the Tellers' farmhouse and found Livi-from-Hawaii sitting there.

Shortly, he'd be handing the farm over to the people he'd hired to look after it and taking the Tellers and Greta to Denver with him, and he had no idea what was going to happen then. Especially when it came to Greta. Raising a kid was so much more involved than anything he'd ever done before. He had to be her *father*. Her family along with the Tellers.

But what did he know about being part of a family? About having a family?

Nothing. Flat-out nothing.

At least nothing good, nothing he wanted to repeat.

And now it was on him to be that, to provide that for Greta.

"I need some help here, guys," he muttered to the memory of Mandy and John Jr.

More help than what his geriatric charges could give, he thought.

And the Tellers liked Livi.

Greta liked Livi.

Plus Maeve was probably right—Greta was going to need the influence and advice of a woman younger than eighty.

He didn't have a wife anymore—he'd already blown that. There was no one else on the docket to fill that bill and take over that duty.

And Livi Camden was applying for the job.

So he guessed that rather than buck the Tellers, rather than deny Greta something she should have and clearly wanted, he supposed he had to give in on this.

Sorry, Mandy, he said mentally to his lost friend. *But I swear I'll stick as close as I can every minute she's with Greta, to keep an eagle eye on her. No matter what, I won't let another Camden hurt somebody you care about.*

Even if it meant he had to take a hard line with Livi down the road, if he discovered she did have some kind of Camden ulterior motive.

Even if it meant he had to be a son of a bitch to her a second time.

He really hoped it didn't come to that. Not with the first woman he'd had the slightest inclination to approach since his divorce.

The woman he'd had on his mind a surprising amount during the last two months.

The woman who had—at first sight this afternoon—made his pulse kick up a notch. And not just out of guilt for how things had been left in Hawaii, but simply from setting eyes on her again.

He had to keep in perspective that that one night in Hawaii was nothing *but* one night. In Hawaii.

Because incredible blue eyes that made his pulse race or not, he couldn't deal with any more than he already was.

Chapter Three

The Camden ranch house was still empty when Livi got back after meeting Greta and the Tellers.

And Callan.

Callan from Hawaii.

She'd driven home in the same dull sense of disbelief that she'd been in since setting eyes on him again. She was glad her cousin Seth wasn't back yet because she needed some time for what had happened to sink in.

She dropped her purse in the foyer, took a sharp right to the living room and sank into one of the oversize leather easy chairs, slumping so low her head rested on the back cushion.

Her mind was spinning.

Callan.

The stranger on the beach in Hawaii was from Denver. With connections in Northbridge. Just like her.

And now they'd met again...

Was the universe toying with her or was she going to wake up and realize she was dreaming this whole thing?

She knew it was just wishful thinking that this was all some kind of nightmare that would fade away as soon as she woke up.

But still she pinched her eyes closed for a minute and then opened them wide.

No, she definitely wasn't dreaming.

And she wasn't nauseous.

That thought almost made her cry.

Because if the nausea was coming from stress, this was the time for it. She should have been miserably sick to her stomach, since the tension she was feeling was through the roof.

But she wasn't feeling queasy.

With the exception of the cooking smells at last week's Sunday-dinner at GiGi's house, she was sick only in the mornings.

Morning sickness.

Her mind wasn't even letting her skirt around it now, as if seeing Callan again made everything more real. Even her memories of Hawaii...

That day had been the ninth anniversary of her wedding to Patrick. The fourth without him. It was still a bad day every year. A day she had to struggle through.

The first year she'd immersed herself in everything she'd had of Patrick's, everything that kept him alive for her. She'd set out every picture she had of him, worn one of his shirts, padded around in his bedroom slippers. She'd gone through everything and anything that reminded her of him. She'd wallowed in all she'd lost and her own misery.

That had been a terrible day.

So the next year she'd tried plunging herself into work, going into the office at six that morning, staying until the cleaning crew showed up that night, pretending it was just business as usual.

But the cleaners had found her sobbing at her desk, because work hadn't made anything better, either.

Last year she'd tried enlisting her family to distract her. And they had. They'd whisked her off to the mountains to go boating and water-skiing on Dillon Lake.

But all she'd been able to think about, to talk about, had been Patrick—how much Patrick had loved days like that with her family, how much he'd loved the water and how often he'd talked about retiring seaside somewhere, how much he'd loved barbecuing...

And by the end of the boating and barbecuing and s'mores, she'd still been a mess.

So this year, in Hawaii, she'd decided to deal with her anniversary by disengaging. By skipping the conference, not scheduling any meetings, any breakfasts, lunches or dinners. By not doing anything.

"Pamper yourself," her sister and Jani had urged, worried about her being so far away and alone on that day.

Taking their recommendation, Livi had slept until she couldn't sleep any more—until after noon, something she never did.

Then she'd gone to the hotel's luxury spa, where she'd had a massage in near silence, not inviting or welcoming any conversation from the masseuse, trying to keep her mind blank.

Afterward the massage therapist had advised her to sit in the sauna, to sweat out the toxins. *You'll feel like a new woman*, she had said.

Livi rarely used the sauna because she wasn't fond of heat like that, but on that day of all days she wanted to feel like a new woman, because feeling like the old one wasn't good. So she'd sat in the sauna, thinking only about how hot it was, about sweating away the old Livi and emerging a new one.

Which she'd actually sort of felt she'd accomplished by the time she'd finished. She'd been so calm and relaxed and...well, just different than she usually felt. Especially on her anniversary.

Different enough to decide to go with the flow of that feeling by moving on to the hotel's salon.

She hadn't had a haircut since Patrick's death. Four years without so much as a trim.

Patrick had liked her hair long and she just hadn't been able to have any of it cut.

But that day she'd actually felt like it. Nothing short, no huge change, nothing Patrick would have even noticed, just a little something...

Which was what she'd done—had a scant two inches cut off the length. But she'd also had the sides feathered, and then agreed to the highlights the stylist suggested.

It was funny how a small change could catapult her even further into feeling like a whole new woman.

And while she was at it, why not go all the way? The makeup artist had had a cancelation and offered Livi his services. Why not have her face done, too?

For Lindie's wedding, Livi had declined the opportunity for that and stuck with her usual subdued blush and mascara. But on that day in Hawaii she'd let the makeup artist go ahead with whatever he wanted to do—nothing dramatic, but different shades of the colors she liked, and slightly more of everything.

And while he'd worked, she'd also let the manicurist do a skin-softening waxing—feet and hands—for which she'd taken off her wedding rings.

By then she'd been all in with the idea of a New Livi for just one day, so she'd had her nails painted bright red and stenciled with white flowery designs—something more showy than she'd ever done before.

She honestly had felt like someone different when she'd left the salon, and she'd decided that maybe doing things she never did was the answer to getting through the anniversary. Certainly it had been helping to keep the sadness away more than anything had before.

And she'd definitely wanted to keep that going.

So she'd left her rings in her purse and splurged in the hotel's dress shop, changing into a halter sundress that exposed so much shoulder that it forced her to include her bra with the bag of clothes she'd had sent to her room.

She'd never been to a bar alone and she *had* chosen the table farthest out on the beach, away from the bar itself and the guests mingling around it, but it was still something the Old Livi would never have done.

And the New Livi had ordered a drink. And then a second one. Because, after all, the sun was low in the sky by then and she'd felt floaty and really, really nice. Really, really as if she were someone else. And that someone else wanted another drink...

It was that someone else who had looked up to find the oh-so-good-looking guy saying hello to her halfway through her second drink. That someone else who had said yes when he'd asked if he could sit with her. That someone else from then on.

Maybe it had been the liquor, but she'd found Callan as easy to talk to as Patrick had always been, and after a while she'd realized that she was having a good time with him. That she was feeling a connection—in the most superficial way, of course—with Callan. A connection she hadn't felt with any man she wasn't related to since Patrick.

And it helped that the only similarity between Callan and her Patrick was that she'd found them both easy to talk to. In every other way, Callan was very different.

Patrick hadn't been too tall—only five-eight. Patrick had not had an athlete's body—he'd been slight, weighing only twenty pounds more than she did.

Patrick's fair hair had been thin, his hairline receding, and he'd had unremarkable, boy-next-door good looks, with his ruddy cheeks and nondescript hazel eyes hidden behind the glasses he'd needed to wear.

It had been Patrick's winning personality that had gained him friends and jobs. And her.

So sitting at that beachside table—and, yes, hitting it off—with a tall, imposing guy with great hair and great eyes and great features, and a body that was not only athletic and hard, but also muscular and broad-shouldered and so, so masculine, had not been something Livi Camden-Walsh was experienced at.

And she most definitely wasn't experienced at not only chatting and laughing with the stranger, but flirting with him, too…

Yes, she'd been flirting with him.

And she'd never flirted with anyone but Patrick in her life.

But her Hawaiian alter ego had actually been good at it. Again, maybe because of the booze.

They'd sat there until late. Until the hula dancing was done. Until the live music ended. Until there were no more than a few people at the bar. She and Callan had sat there drinking and talking about nothing that meant anything.

Finally, Livi noticed that the moon was high, and decided it must be late and she should call it a night.

No, not yet—how about a walk on the beach? he'd said.

Any other time, any other man and she wouldn't have let him postpone her exit.

But that night, her Hawaiian alter ego had taken Callan's hand when he'd held it out to her to help her from her chair.

Then they'd walked on the beach side by side in the moonlight, laughing and flirting. And the farther up the beach they'd gone, the more removed she'd felt from everything but the beauty of that tropical paradise and that man who continued to bring her out of herself.

She was so much out-of-herself and so completely inhabiting her Hawaiian alter ego that when she stumbled and Callan caught her arm to keep her from falling, she hadn't minded.

And when that hand had stayed on her arm, when she'd looked up into that handsome face to make a joke about her clumsiness, she remembered well that he'd been looking down at her with a thoughtful smile and eyes that seemed too gentle for someone so big and manly.

She'd been lost in what she'd seen in those eyes, and when he'd kissed her, it wasn't as if he was kissing Livi Camden-Walsh, it was as if he was kissing someone else. And she was just getting to enjoy it.

And she *had* enjoyed it. He had a way about him, a technique, that was so…well, just so good that it drew her even further out of herself, forgetting about everything but that kissing that washed her mind of all other thoughts and carried her away.

She wasn't even surprised when she found herself kissing him back with just as much heat.

And from that moment on—until she woke up alone in his bed hours and hours later—she really, truly didn't feel that she was Livi Camden-Walsh. She was totally that someone else she'd set out to be after the sauna. That someone who got to forget herself and escape how much it hurt every time she thought about Patrick being gone.

That someone who had been sinking into a sated slumber when Callan had told her that the condom had broken *just a little*, so she hadn't worried about it…

She wished that that had woken her fully, bringing her back to herself…but it hadn't. She'd fallen asleep as that new person who didn't worry, didn't fuss, didn't grieve.

But she'd woken up as herself at four in the morning, horrified and ashamed.

At first she'd worried about how she was going to face Callan. Wherever he was—the bathroom maybe? As she'd dressed, she'd thought about the conversation she needed to have with him. She would explain that she hadn't been herself, that normally she was the last person to ever even consider having a vacation fling. And then she'd say that it would be best if they just went their separate ways. When she'd finished perfecting the words in her head, she'd walked over to tap on the bathroom door…but it had swung open under her touch, revealing that there was no one inside.

It was then that she'd started to realize that the whole place was too silent for anyone else to be in it.

She'd paused to actually look around, and discovered that Callan was gone.

It was four in the morning and he was gone. There was no note, no explanation. She tried to come up with excuses for him. Maybe he'd gone out for a cigarette, or to get some ice. But his teeth were too white for him to be a smoker, and the ice bucket was still on the bar. Nothing was open in the hotel at that hour, so he couldn't have gone to one of the restaurants or bars.

Still, she'd waited five minutes for him to get back from wherever he'd gone. Then ten. Then half an hour. By the time an hour had ticked by, she couldn't bear to wait any longer.

Livi had no experience with any of this, but she had friends who had talked about guys sneaking out once the deed was done, and she'd suddenly felt certain that that had to be what had gone on with Callan. She'd pictured him slinking out so as not to wake her and hiding somewhere. In the room of a friend, maybe? They hadn't talked about anything personal, so she had no idea if he was at the hotel alone or with other people. People he could take refuge with until she was gone.

All she'd wanted to do was get out of there, get to her own room, shower and call the airline to change her ticket so she could go home a day early.

Home, where she could write off that night to pure and utter insanity, and resolve never to think about it again.

As she'd left his suite she'd dug in her tiny purse for her wedding rings and put them back on with a vengeance. She'd just been grateful that what she'd done had happened far away from her loved ones, who would never need to know.

She'd also been grateful that she'd never have to see that guy again or be reminded of him in any way.

And she'd sworn to herself that she would never, ever, ever even wish to forget herself like that again.

Sitting in the big leather chair in the ranch's living room now, she groaned.

It had been such a good plan...

Until she'd missed her first period.

And now her second.

Until the nausea had started.

And her fingers had swelled too much to wear her rings.

It had been such a good plan, until she'd seen Callan again today...

The front door opened just then and her cousin Seth came in, calling her name.

"I'm right here," Livi answered, her voice weak as she opened her eyes once more.

But she couldn't let Seth think anything was wrong, so she got up from the chair and pasted on a smile.

"Hey there!" Seth greeted her, coming with open arms to hug her. "Sorry I had to be gone when you got here."

"You're here now," she said feebly, wishing he wasn't, that he had stayed in Texas, where she knew he'd left his wife and baby to visit longer with his father-in-law.

"I'm here, but kicking myself because I just remembered that I have a Cattlemen's Association dinner tonight and I'm gonna have to turn around and leave again."

There was some relief in hearing that. She had too much on her mind to socialize even with her cousin, who was like a brother to her.

"Don't worry about it. Do whatever you need to do. I'm fine on my own."

"There's plenty of food in the fridge, or if you want

to wait until I get back around eight I can bring you a pizza or something."

"I'll find something in the fridge. I was going to go to bed early, anyway."

"Tomorrow, then…"

Livi nodded, again not altogether tuned in to what was going on. "I promised to pick up my new charge, Greta Teller, after school tomorrow, and I was going to go to the store in town before that for a few things I didn't pack. But I'm free until about two or so."

"I meet with my ranch hands on Monday mornings to schedule out the week, but how about lunch?"

Which would give her time to stop being sick.

Unless she woke up tomorrow with her period and without the nausea, and everything was okay…

Apparently she still had a little denial left.

"Lunch would be good," she said.

With that settled, Seth dragged his suitcase in from the foyer and began to rummage in the side pockets. "So you must have found the Tellers' farm without me," he said.

"Yeah, I did. I just got back from there a few minutes ago."

"You met everyone? The Tellers and their granddaughter? The guardian?"

"Callan Tierney," she informed him.

That halted the search and Seth glanced up at her with arched eyebrows. "*Callan Tierney* is the girl's guardian? You know who he is, don't you?"

"Why would I know who he is?"

Seth went back to searching through his bag, but said, "I've never met him, but Callan Tierney is CT Software. *We* use his software and so do a slew of other businesses around the world. He's worth more than we are. I wonder how someone like him ended up the guardian of a kid in Northbridge?"

"I don't know," Livi said honestly.

"Ah, that's what I need for tonight!" Seth exclaimed, pulling a tablet out of the suitcase. Then, turning back to her, he said, "You'll have to fill me in when you find out."

"Sure. When I find out," she parroted.

Seth continued chatting with her, telling her about his time away. Livi did her best to keep up with that conversation. But she was still reeling inside and thinking more about the next day than anything he was saying.

The next day, when she would go into town before picking up Greta Teller.

When she would take the first step to putting denial to rest once and for all.

And buy a home pregnancy test.

After lunch with Seth on Monday, and a solo trip to the personal care section of Northbridge's general store that made Livi cringe inside, she picked up Greta from the local school.

The little girl was wearing the scarf Livi had given her the day before, and immediately asked her to tie it "better" because on the playground Jake Linman had pulled on it.

Livi obliged her as Greta launched into another outpouring of admiration for the ballet flats Livi was wearing today, the small leather cross-body purse she was using and the pin-tucked white blouse she had on over a pale blue tank top with navy blue slacks.

But Livi was only partially listening. Her mind was still on that pregnancy test and the results it might show when she took it.

"There you go," she said when the scarf was retied.

"Dumb Jake Linman," Greta grumbled. "He's always bothering me."

"Maybe he likes you. Sometimes that's how boys show it," Livi responded without much thought.

"That's what my gramma says," Greta said, as if she was hoping for something else from Livi. Then she added under her breath, "Doesn't matter. Tomorrow is my last day."

The last day for what? Livi wondered, before remembering that Greta was being made to move to Denver. That meant leaving her school, her friends, the town that was home to her.

And Livi had been thinking so much about her own problems that she hadn't recognized Greta's.

But that's the reason I'm here! she chastised herself.

She genuinely liked this little girl now that she'd met her, and not only had GiGi assigned her this make-amends project, Livi honestly wanted to help.

So regardless of what was going on in her own life, when she was with Greta, it had to be all about the girl, she realized. She had to take her own problems out of the picture. Greta had to be the center of things.

Which was exactly what Livi did for the remainder of the afternoon as she bought her ice cream and then a pair of new shoes and a matching purse that Greta admired in a shop window.

Apparently new shoes and a new purse had the same effect on little girls as big ones, because by the end of the afternoon Greta was in better spirits, and Livi felt as if she'd done some good.

It was after five when she drove up the dirt lane to

the Tellers' house, passing a truck loaded with bales of hay going in the opposite direction.

She could see Callan in the barn behind the house and that was when her vow to focus only on Greta hit a snag. One look at him and Livi stopped hearing what her young charge was saying.

He was rearranging hay bales, pivoting back and forth, facing her, then facing away.

She wasn't sure if Callan hadn't noticed her arrival or if he was merely ignoring it, but he didn't so much as look in her direction.

And that gave her the opportunity to watch him freely for a moment.

Like the day before, he was dressed in boots, jeans and a work shirt—this one plaid flannel. He looked every inch the cowboy, all rugged and strong. And watching him, she found it hard to think he was anything *but* a cowboy.

The weather was warm and he had the sleeves of his shirt rolled above his elbows, leaving a hint of biceps and impressive forearms bare to where suede gloves encased big hands. She could see the shift of muscles as he hoisted the bales. Muscles like nothing she'd ever seen in any other computer whiz.

Long legs braced the weight, with thick thighs testing the denim of his jeans. His shoulders were broad and straight and seemed more likely forged by backbreaking farm work than sitting behind a desk.

And that face that had so impressed her alter ego in Hawaii—clean-shaven that evening—was made only sexier with a scruff of day's beard shadowing his sharp jawline, making him look just gritty enough to be a turn-on.

Not that she was turned on. Livi was clear about that.

But still, there was no looking at Callan, watching him do what he was doing, without appreciating the undeniable appeal of a fit man's physique.

In a purely analytical way.

Until her traitorous brain zoomed somewhere else.

Back to Hawaii. To that night. She'd insisted on complete darkness, so she hadn't really seen him naked.

Something she suddenly regretted...

She realized belatedly that she'd completely missed whatever it was that Greta was talking about. She tuned back in as the child unfastened her seat belt and opened the car door, saying, "Let's go show Uncle Callan my new stuff!"

Oh.

Livi swallowed and got a grip on herself, coming totally into the present again.

What do I do now? she thought.

What was the protocol for two people in this situation? *Was* there a protocol?

Yesterday had been awkward, but there had been the Tellers and the nurse and Greta to serve as a buffer between her and Callan, plus so much going on that they'd both addressed only what was happening.

But now? If she followed Greta to the barn—as it seemed she should—then what?

Did they just go on acting like strangers?

Or did they, at some point, talk about Hawaii?

Did she tell him what a jerk she thought he was for ditching her in the middle of the night after sleeping with him?

Or was she supposed to act as if it hadn't fazed her? As if it was par for the course—sleep together, go your separate ways, it happened all the time...

Was that what he thought of her? That she slept around so much that it wouldn't be any big deal for a guy to slip out after the fact, without a word? That that *was* a common occurrence to her?

What an awful thought.

It made her want to shout that until him she'd slept with only one man in her life: Patrick. The man she'd loved and been devoted to. The man who had loved and been devoted to her. Her soul mate and the person she'd expected to spend her entire life with.

But if she did shout that she would just sound defensive, and Callan probably wouldn't even believe it.

What *did* people do in a situation like this?

For the second time in two days Livi just wanted to hide or run the other way.

But by then Greta had reached the barn and alerted Callan to the fact that they were there, and he was looking straight at Livi across the distance.

She took a deep breath and decided that, at any rate, she wasn't going to act as if she'd done something wrong.

Yes, she *felt* like she'd done something wrong—something terribly wrong—by sleeping with him, but in spite of that, people *did* hook up with someone they'd just met for one-night stands.

If anyone should be embarrassed, it should be him, for the way he'd treated her—slithering silently out like a snake.

If either of them needed to hang their head in shame, it was him!

So she got out of the car and followed Greta's path to the barn.

She had barely exchanged hellos with Callan when the little girl announced that she was going to show her grandparents her new shoes and purse. Thinking of that as a reprieve, Livi turned to follow.

Until Callan said, "Can you hang back, Livi?"

And off went Greta. Leaving Livi alone with this man she'd never wanted to see again as long as she lived.

"I wanted to talk to you yesterday, but then I had to come out and load that truck. John Sr. won't let me let anything slide..." Callan stopped short, as if to keep himself from saying more on that subject, and then started again. "And before I got back inside, you were gone. But we do need to talk."

"Okay," Livi said, with a note of challenge creeping into her tone. She was unwilling to give him any help.

"Hawaii..." he said. "I need to apologize to you for that."

For the night they'd spent together? Or for leaving?

She raised her chin and gazed at him.

"My phone was on vibrate, so it woke me but not you a couple of hours after we fell asleep."

Livi had thought yesterday was awkward, but this had it beat.

"I definitely didn't hear anything," she said with accusation in her voice, thinking that he was just making up some excuse.

"The call was to let me know that Greta's parents, J.J.—John Jr.—and Mandy, had been in a car accident here," he said, knocking some of the wind out of Livi's sails. "Mandy had died on impact. J.J. was still alive but in critical condition. No one was giving him much time..."

Callan's deep voice got more and more ragged as he spoke, and Livi could see that even now this was difficult for him.

And she'd thought that *she* was the one entitled to the emotions…

For the second time today she had to make an adjustment, suspend her own feelings and just listen.

"I had to get to J.J.," he went on. "I had to make sure everything that *could* be done for him *was* being done. I had to see him…"

Callan cleared his throat, and realizing how hard-hit he still was somehow made Livi feel guilty for all the nasty things she'd thought about him and his impromptu departure from that hotel room.

"Mandy, J.J. and I grew up here together," he explained. "We were close. And always stayed close. They were more family to me than my own…"

As if he needed a diversion, he looked down at his hands and pulled off his gloves, slapping them against his thigh.

And Livi hated that her brain was once again thinking about how glorious those hands and thighs were. What in the world was wrong with her?

"So when I got that call," he continued, "I was only thinking about getting to J.J. Everything went to that. I was in the air an hour later, and halfway here before I realized—"

That not even a thought of her had entered his mind? That fact still stung, even though he'd had a good reason to be otherwise occupied.

"—that I'd just rushed out on you without a word," he was saying. "By then, when I called the hotel, you were out of the room. And since I didn't even know your last name, I didn't have any way to track you down. I did try, I swear to you…" He paused, then added, "Anyway, I'm sorry."

Livi raised her chin a second time, accepting the apology that way because she couldn't *not* accept it when it came with that explanation.

But it wasn't easy to let go of the humiliation she'd felt at his vanishing without a trace. It was hard to move past thinking the worst of him.

Instead she chose to say quietly, "I'm sorry about your friends."

He nodded solemnly. "Yeah. Me, too. They were good people."

Again he didn't seem to want to make eye contact with her, instead turning to toss the gloves onto a hay bale. "Anyway," he repeated, "here we are."

"Here we are," Livi echoed.

"And I thought maybe we should talk about...you know...where we go now."

He did meet her eyes then and Livi didn't allow herself to look away. But she didn't say anything, because she had no idea where they *should* go now—especially factoring in that pregnancy test she had in that bag in the trunk of her cousin's car.

"How about we just put it behind us?" Callan suggested. "Forget it happened. Start fresh."

Easy for him to say.

"You want to help Greta," he went on, "and now she's kind of my job—her and the Tellers—so we'll be seeing each other. But Hawaii was...well..."

A one-night stand? A vacation fling? Pure stupidity on her part? Yes, what exactly should they call it?

As bad as the last two months had been for Livi, this was worse. This was excruciating. It felt like a brush-off. As if he was telling her that even though they'd slept together, he didn't want there to be anything more between them than that.

And while she certainly didn't, either, it was still a rejection. This made it seem as if she expected something from him that he was letting her know he wasn't on board for.

I belong to Patrick! she wanted to tell him in no uncertain terms.

But she resisted the urge. Instead, she tried to rise above what felt like an insult and said, "Hawaii is already forgotten."

Liar, liar, pants on fire...

"And we can just do...whatever...for Greta and go on?" Callan asked.

"Sure."

"Not that Hawaii wasn't something damn memorable..." he said, as if giving credit where credit was due, his eyebrows raised in what looked like appreciation.

"But it's over and done with. Finished. On to a new chapter," she said curtly.

This time it was Callan who nodded in acknowledgment. "Yeah, I guess," he said, though now he sounded a little confused. And perhaps a little offended. "But maybe we should actually get to know each other...for Greta's sake."

Was that what he'd been trying to say? Livi didn't have any experience with any of this, and was running on high-octane emotions. Maybe he wasn't being a jerk—even if it still felt that way.

She took a deep breath and tried to look at things from a calmer, less sensitive perspective.

She'd been as responsible as he had been for them

spending the night together in Hawaii. And though he had left, he'd had a good reason.

Now here they were, but he'd inherited a nine-year-old—and apparently two geriatrics on top of it—and had his hands full. It stood to reason that romance was the last thing he needed at the moment. And yet he and Livi would still have to spend time together, for Greta's sake, so it made sense to settle things between them.

And it wasn't as if her own thinking was any different than it had been before she'd met him in Hawaii. Livi still couldn't imagine herself in a relationship with anyone other than Patrick.

Take away her newest worry, and Callan was right that they just needed to wrap up Hawaii and stuff it in a compartment. That they just needed to start over as nothing more than they actually were—two strangers brought together over the welfare of a little girl.

Thinking about it all like that helped Livi calm down.

"Hawaii is history," she decreed. "Let's wipe the slate clean and just move on."

Those words again. Only it was her saying them this time.

But in this instance she meant them. She just hoped that they *could* move on freely and with a genuinely clean slate. If they couldn't—if that pregnancy test came back positive... But she refused to think about that yet. She'd wait to deal with that hurdle when she'd actually taken the test and knew for sure what was going on.

There was certainly no need to tell Callan before then.

"So we're okay?" he asked, sounding sincere.

"We're okay," Livi confirmed, with more bravado than confidence.

"Good," he said, as if he was relieved.

"Good," she parroted, not relieved at all. Then she inclined her head toward the house, told him she needed to get going and wanted to say goodbye to Greta.

"Sure," Callan said, bending over to pick up those gloves, putting them on again.

Onto those hands that Livi suddenly recalled the feel of on her body.

Until she forced that memory out of her head, took a long pull of fresh air and turned to go to the farmhouse.

Chapter Four

It was positive.

Livi took the home pregnancy test first thing Tuesday morning and stared at the display on the stick until it showed the results.

But a positive reading didn't *necessarily* mean the test was right.

There were false positives, weren't there?

Or she could have done it wrong.

Dazed, feeling as if everything was spinning out of control, she reread the instructions.

Then she stared at the display again, willing it to show her something different.

And at the same time thinking that this would have been such happy news if Patrick was still alive.

They'd wanted children, had tried for them. She'd even had a plan for how to tell him.

But this?

She just couldn't face it happening like this.

So she wasn't going to, she decided.

She wasn't going to fully believe it until a doctor told her for sure.

Especially when she was hardly sick at all this morning.

She'd go to the doctor. The doctor would say this happened sometimes—an imbalance of hormones that was delaying her period and causing a false-positive test, but she wasn't pregnant.

She couldn't be pregnant.

The doctor would clear it all up.

The sooner the better.

So she called her gynecologist in Denver and made an appointment, trying desperately to stay in a state of denial.

Livi was surprised—and not particularly pleased—to find Callan at Greta's school when she went for Greta's going-away party that afternoon.

Greta had invited her the day before, but hadn't mentioned that Callan was coming, too. And Livi was in no shape to see him—the guy who wanted them both to just forget Hawaii and everything that had happened there.

How would she ever tell *him*?

But she couldn't think about it. She couldn't think about any of it. And she'd given herself permission not to until she saw her doctor, so she pushed any notion of pregnancy out of her mind.

What she couldn't push out of her mind, though, was Callan himself.

They were sitting on the side of the room, Callan

slightly ahead of her, just enough in her line of vision to distract her from what the teacher was saying about how much they would all miss Greta.

He was dressed more the way he'd been in Hawaii—in khakis and a navy blue polo shirt. But he couldn't have looked more uncomfortable, sitting like a giant in the too-small-for-him desk chair.

It wasn't only the chair, though. Even as the party got under way Livi could see how much of a fish out of water he was when it came to kids, Greta included.

The day before, when Greta had run to him in the barn, Livi had lagged behind, so she'd seen very little of the exchange between them. And on Sunday, when she'd witnessed his unenthusiastic response to Greta's delight in the scarf, Livi had thought that was due to his shock at seeing her.

But he wasn't any different at the going-away party. He was still wooden and overly formal, as if someone had set him down in a room full of aliens and he just didn't know how to relate.

It made Livi begin to wonder about him as the choice to raise Greta.

Or any child…

After the party Greta begged Livi to come back to the farm and stay for dinner with the family.

She didn't have the heart to say no, when saying goodbye to her friends had clearly left the little girl down in the dumps. The only thing that seemed to perk her up was the idea of Livi coming home with her so Greta could show her the mementos and going-away gifts her friends had given her.

So Livi accepted.

Over dinner she saw more of what she'd glimpsed only

a hint of on Sunday—a certain tension in the dynamic between Callan and John Sr.

Maeve Teller seemed to be fond of Callan. In fact, she doted on him the way she might have doted on a son. The thin, slight woman with the gaunt face and long, silver hair wound into a bun at her nape was warm and loving toward Callan.

John Sr. was another story. He was a big man—tall and boxy, with only a wreath of white hair remaining around a bald center, and a face that resembled a bulldog. There was nothing lighthearted about him in any way, but to Maeve and Greta he was gruffly loving. When it came to Callan, he was only gruff.

The two men didn't speak to each other unless it was necessary. Callan was strictly civil, but John Sr. bordered on rude, never looking at him without a scowl. Most of what he did say to Callan seemed to hint that he only expected the worst from him, that he didn't like or trust him.

It was understandable that Callan didn't appreciate it, and easy to see his negative feelings in response. But he tolerated John Sr.'s treatment of him without striking back, and Livi wasn't quite sure what to make of that. Certainly her impression of Callan was not as someone who would just accept such scorn and contempt.

After the meal there was a joint cleanup involving Livi, Callan, Greta and Kinsey, before Livi announced that she had to go. She was flying back to Denver before dawn in order to get to her doctor—though she only said she had an early flight, without giving the reason why.

Greta wanted her to stay, but Maeve and Callan both reminded the little girl that the next day was a travel day for them, too, and that she needed to get to bed.

Because the house had not even begun to be packed up, Livi was surprised to hear that they would be following so soon, but she assured the child that she would see her in Denver.

Then, although there was no need for it, Callan walked Livi out to her car.

"Do you have movers coming tomorrow?" Livi asked along the way to satisfy her own curiosity.

"The house is staying intact—I've hired a man and his wife to move in and take care of it and the farm for now, until the Tellers decide whether or not they want to sell. In Denver, they'll be living with me, too, so there's no reason to bring anything but what they need or want for themselves for now. My pilot flew in today and came out here to take what belongings the Tellers wanted with them to make their room feel like home, suitcases were mostly packed today to go out tomorrow with us, so we're all set."

"Oh," Livi muttered. She'd thought that she would have a little break from him, a little time to get her bearings at home before contending with everything. But she guessed not.

"Kinsey is driving in ahead of us tomorrow—her car is here, so she can't fly back with us," he was saying as they drew near Livi's borrowed sedan. "She'll be in Denver around noon and will go straight to my place to arrange accommodations for Maeve's wheelchair. Any chance you could meet her there and—I don't know— take a look at the room that will be Greta's? Maybe do a little something? A decorator handled everything, so it isn't all pink and frilly the way her room at home is, or even the way Maeve has her room here."

"Two things," Livi said in response to the request. "I

can't redecorate a room in a couple of hours. And I think it's a better idea to let Greta make the changes. It'll help it feel more like her room if she chooses the bedspread and curtains and anything that goes up on the walls. What I *can* do is maybe have some new stuffed animals and dolls waiting for her, so the space seems more welcoming. And once she's in town, I'd be happy to take her shopping for more things."

"Just the two of you…" he said, more to himself than to her. He seemed to consider that for a moment and then he let out an almost inaudible sigh that gave Livi the sense there were still reservations in his feelings about her being with Greta. But still he said, "Yeah, okay, I guess that would be good. Tomorrow—and the whole move—is going to be a big deal for all of them and I'm just trying to figure out how to make it easier."

When they reached Livi's car she opened the door but didn't get in. She was wondering about too many things from her afternoon and evening watching his interactions with all three Tellers. And since he'd wandered out here with her and the evening air was still warm—and he didn't seem to be in any hurry for her to leave—she thought she'd take the opportunity to do a little digging.

"You don't seem all that comfortable with…things," she ventured.

"Things?"

"Greta, being around kids…and John Sr., too. Did you know you were being named as Greta's guardian?" Livi asked, narrowing the scope of her inquiry to that for starters.

"Sure, I knew. Mandy and J.J. asked me if I'd do it. But you know, you never think anything is actually going to happen."

"And now that it has? Is it a job you really want?"

His brows drew down over those brooding, coffee-colored eyes, but he didn't hesitate to say, "I wouldn't have it any other way."

That surprised her. "It's just that you don't seem..." She struggled for a diplomatic way to express what she was thinking. "You aren't married anymore and don't have any kids of your own, if I'm remembering what you said in Hawaii—"

"Just before *you* said you weren't married—anymore—and didn't have any kids, either, and then told me you didn't want to talk about our real lives," he stated drily.

She needed fewer and fewer reminders of that night, as more and more details popped into her head every time she was with him.

But she stayed on track and said, "So you're a single guy without any experience with children, let alone a little girl. Yet they chose you as Greta's guardian."

"And you can't figure out why they would have," he surmised with a wry laugh and a hint of a smile that lifted one side of his mouth.

"I'm just wondering about it, is all."

"I grew up here," he said, nodding in the general direction of Northbridge. "On the wrong side of the tracks. My father's family had a good-sized working farm at one point, but when my old man inherited it he let everything go to seed, then sold it off acre by acre for booze money for him and my mother."

That was blunt and raised Livi's eyebrows. "Your parents had a drinking problem," she said, putting it in more polite terms.

"They didn't think it was a problem. For them, it was a way of life. They drank from the minute their feet hit the floor in the morning until they passed out. And when they came to, they drank more."

"Did they do that from when you were just a little kid?"

"I think they always drank, yeah—my mother even admitted that she drank some when she was pregnant with me. I can recall knowing as a little kid that there was my orange juice for breakfast and *grown-up* orange juice that I wasn't supposed to touch."

"You actually remember that?"

"I do," he said without question, before picking up where he'd left off. "But they held jobs until I was maybe seven or eight, so I guess they were initially what's considered 'functional alcoholics'—they'd just hit the bottle hardest after work. But they got less and less functional and kept losing their jobs. By the time I was about Greta's age, drinking was pretty much their occupation."

"But they still took care of you," Livi said, assuming that had to be true.

"In their way," he answered with a shrug. "The more they drank, the more I took care of them. But luckily, as that started to happen, I was old enough to do things for myself."

"Everything?" Livi asked, unable to imagine that a nine- or ten-year-old could take complete care of himself and his parents, too.

Callan looked embarrassed to admit it, but said, "I have a pretty high IQ and I guess that was to my advantage in more than my schoolwork. And this is the country—kids aren't pampered out here. They have to pitch in at an early age. For me, by the time I was in fifth grade, it wasn't feeding chickens or slopping hogs before school, it was fixing breakfast and getting my parents to eat, or dragging clothes to the Laundromat while they were buying liquor and cigarettes and groceries—"

"So they *did* buy groceries."

"Yeah, they did. I'd make a list for them—canned soup and beans, frozen dinners, bread, peanut butter. Stuff for meals I could manage myself, plus things like toilet paper and soap."

"Would they have only bought the liquor if you hadn't made them a list for the other stuff?"

"More than likely. They didn't really care about food. If I didn't make dinner, they didn't eat, just drank. I did the dishes—when there weren't any more clean ones. Brought cash to town to pay to keep our utilities on. Wrote my own notes for school and forged their signatures. I just kept things going—not great, but the best I could as a kid."

He didn't say that with any self-pity, his tone matter-of-fact.

"No one called Social Services?" Livi asked.

"It wasn't as if my parents ever physically hurt me, so there wasn't that to trigger anything. They loved me in their way. Booze was just their priority and I had to adapt."

Their priority over him.

That was so sad.

"Every year my father would sell off another acre or two of land and we'd live off that money. We had enough to get by, and I kept my mouth shut about what my home life was like."

"So no intervention?"

"No intervention. I guess I did just enough to dodge that bullet. But I wasn't the most popular person around," he said. "I was still the poor kid who lived out in a run-down trailer and wore secondhand clothes. That didn't put me on the guest list to many birthday parties. Most parents didn't want their kids around that kind of trash."

Was that something he'd heard said about himself? The thought made Livi feel even worse for him, for the little boy he'd been.

"But that didn't faze Mandy and J.J.," Callan concluded in a happier tone. "Don't ask me why, because I couldn't tell you, but Mandy and J.J. were friends to me in spite of what other kids and the rest of the town thought. From kindergarten on, we were stuck together like glue. The three of us."

Livi was leaning back against the car, listening raptly, and Callan moved forward to cross his arms over the top of the open door between them as he went on reminiscing. His striking face was relaxed now, his small smile at the memory of his friends not at all tight or forced.

"The three of us were together through elementary school, middle school, high school, even college—the University of Colorado. I finished my bachelor's degree in three years, then got my master's and graduated a little ahead of them. But the three of us shared a crummy apartment in Boulder—even after they discovered they liked each other as more than friends. I was best man at their wedding."

"You stayed living with newlyweds?" Livi asked.

"Sharing the space made the rent low enough that I could concentrate on developing software without worrying about anything else. So I could put every ounce of time and energy and everything I had into that, and then into the company I founded—CT Software. They just shuffled around me while I monopolized the computer we shared. Sometimes they had more faith in me than I had in myself."

That made Livi think of Patrick, who had seen more in her than she'd known she was capable of.

"Once things started to go my way and I launched the company," Callan went on, "there was no question that Mandy and J.J. should be in on it with me. I wanted them to be partners, but they wouldn't do that—not when I was funding it with the money I made from selling off the last acre of land that belonged to my family. But they let me make them my vice presidents and put them on the business side of things so we could work together every day. Which was great!" He said that with so much satisfaction.

"But when Greta came along, they wanted to raise her in Northbridge, where her grandparents were," he said then. "So we put a marketing and distribution center here for them to run."

"It must have been hard for you to lose them back to Northbridge."

"Yeah. But after they moved, a day never went by that we didn't talk or video chat or text."

"The Tellers said you're Greta's godfather," Livi murmured, beginning to understand the reasons behind J.J and Mandy's choice of guardian. It was more about their close-knit friendship than about Callan's relationship with their daughter.

"I am her godfather," he confirmed. "But because Mandy and J.J. were in Northbridge, I didn't spend a lot of time with Greta until now. Still, Mandy and J.J. had faith that I could and would step up to the plate for her, for them, if I needed to. And I will."

Livi could tell that he meant it, and she had to admire his determination and dedication to his friends.

She just had the impression that he wasn't quite sure how to "step up to the plate" when it came to Greta. But there wasn't anything more for Livi to say about that except, "So you'll work on it?"

He laughed—something she'd heard a lot that night in Hawaii. The sound made a wave of warmth wash through her.

"That's your way of saying I'm not doing well?" he asked.

"There's room for improvement."

He laughed again. "Okay. You want to be my mentor, too?"

A sweet sort of cockiness and a hint of challenge—there had been some of that in Hawaii, too, and Livi found herself smiling. "It's not like I'm an expert, but you—"

"Yeah, I know," he conceded. "I'm a computer nerd, not a kindergarten teacher."

There was absolutely nothing nerdy about him, but Livi didn't point that out. And she wished she wasn't so aware of just how not nerdy he was. In fact, maybe if he was more of a geek it would have kept her from falling under his spell. Which she felt a little like she was doing again, and was trying to fight.

What she did say was a goading, "You do know that Greta isn't in kindergarten, right?"

He laughed once more. "Yeah, I know that much. But it doesn't mean I know how to talk to her."

"How about just like you'd talk to anyone else? Like you're talking to me right now."

His expression revealed he wasn't sure he could do that.

"Just give it a try. Greta is a chatterbox. If you give her half a chance she'll do most of the work."

"She does kind of like to talk, doesn't she?"

It was Livi's turn to laugh. "She's a nine-year-old girl and has a lot to say. But I think you can keep up," she teased.

They'd been out here talking for a long time, so she knew she should say good-night. But Livi was still curious about the tension between Callan and John Sr.—who, according to Maeve, Callan wanted to "look after."

And now that she had him talking about these things, Livi hated to stop before she had the whole scoop.

So—not because she was enjoying standing here in the moonlight talking to him, but for legitimate other reasons, she assured herself—she said, "And the Tellers? Are you taking them with you to Denver to keep them close to Greta?"

"Let me guess—you saw that there was no love lost between me and John Sr., and you want to know about that, too."

Livi hadn't thought she was that transparent. But before she had the chance to respond, he warned, "It's another long story."

"I'd still like to know," she admitted.

He took a deep breath and sighed, seeming more reluctant to get into this one. "Mandy's folks have both passed, so the Tellers are the only grandparents Greta has left, and yeah, keeping them a part of her life the way Mandy and J.J. wanted them to be is a little of it."

"But not all."

"No," he confirmed. "By the time I got here from Hawaii, J.J. was at the end and he knew it…" Callan's voice cracked.

Livi understood all too well how hard it was to talk about people dearly loved and lost.

He cleared his throat. "J.J. was all Maeve and John Sr. had. He asked me to take over for him, to take care of them. I promised I would and I will. But there's more to it than that promise... I also owe them."

"You owe them?" Livi repeated.

"When my parents died—"

"When was that?"

"The end of my junior year in high school."

"Oh. I was thinking it was more recent, but you were just a kid," she said in surprise.

"I don't think I was ever much of a kid even before that. But I wasn't eighteen," he said ominously.

"They died together? Driving drunk?" she guessed.

He shook his head. "They *did* drive drunk—they did everything drunk. It's just lucky that around here it's mostly open country roads without a lot of other cars to get in the way. But no, they weren't in a car accident. They died in a trailer fire."

She hadn't expected that.

"Mandy and J.J. and I had stayed after school to work on a project," Callan said. "It was already too late when the fire department got there—in fact, that whole last acre around the trailer was on fire by then, because without any close neighbors it took somebody spotting the smoke in the distance to call it in. But investigators pinpointed the origin to inside the trailer, at the spot where my father's chair was. I figured my old man had probably passed out with a lit cigarette in his hand.

"And then...there was nothing," Callan concluded with a sad wryness. "I didn't have parents. I didn't have a place to live. All I had was an after-school job at the computer-repair shop. I didn't make enough to support myself."

"I'm so sorry…" Livi said, almost regretting that she'd gotten them into this now.

He didn't address her condolences, but went on matter-of-factly again. "I was seventeen. Going into the foster system would have just been weird at that point—I was mostly grown and I'd been taking care of myself and my parents for years. But I had no resources. All that was left of my family's land was the acre the trailer was on—but it was too charred from fire damage for farming or raising livestock, and would take years to be usable again. It looked like I was going to have to drop out and get full-time work, but then J.J.—and Maeve—went to bat for me. They pleaded with John Sr. to let me move in for that last year. He didn't want to do it—he'd never liked that J.J. was friends with me. And a couple of months before that I'd used J.J.'s computer to hack into the school's system to play a dumb prank that had wreaked a lot of havoc—"

"Uh-oh…"

"Yeah… I was a kid without any supervision—no curfew, no rules and a brain that was always working and not always on the right path," he acknowledged. "Anyway, the prank was traced back to J.J.'s computer and he got the blame. I set it right, even reversed what I'd done so I didn't get kicked out of school, but John Sr. had always been pretty down on me, and that had soured things more."

"With him, but not with Maeve?"

"She had a soft spot for me—something I was grate-ful for but never really understood. She teamed up with J.J. to lean on John Sr. and he finally gave in. Under the condition that I toe the line, keep my after-school job and still earn my keep working on the farm before school the way J.J. did."

"And you did."

"It wasn't something I could pass up. It was just for a year, and then I'd be headed to college—if I could get the scholarships lined up." He again nodded toward Northbridge, adding a heartfelt and desperate sounding, "And I wanted out of this town! So yeah, I did."

"Which let you finish high school and win the scholarship you needed."

"So I owe the Tellers."

"Even if you still haven't quite redeemed yourself in John Sr.'s eyes for some reason..." Livi said, hoping for an explanation of that.

But all she got was stoicism from Callan. "That's just how he is. And that's how I got here."

"So between the two things—your friend asking you to take care of his parents and you owing Maeve and John Sr.—you don't fight the way he treats you," Livi said.

"I won't let down J.J. and Mandy on anything. Not with Greta and not with John Sr.," Callan concluded with resignation.

Then he smiled, warmly enough to remind Livi of some of what had appealed to her in Hawaii, and said, "So, Hawaii is history—we're all the way into real life now, like it or not."

If only you knew...

The moon had gone high into the sky as they'd talked. The way its light caught the sharp lines of Callan's face made her think about their walk on the beach, when he'd first kissed her.

He was looking into her eyes just like he had been that

night. Uninvited and unwanted came a memory of that first kiss they'd shared—how instinctively she'd been drawn to it, how warm and gentle his lips had been.

She remembered thinking as she'd melted into the kiss that there was something indescribably good about the feel of that big body curving almost protectively down toward her in order to reach her mouth with his. About the pure size and power of the man himself—strong but reserved, silently inviting her in—that had added to the potency and made it impossible for her to resist drifting closer to him, to that kiss…

Then she realized what she was thinking about and how inappropriate it was.

And how she most surely shouldn't be having the absolutely insane urge to reexperience it!

She took a deep breath to clear her head and said, "I should go. Pack. Get ready to leave in the morning."

He didn't stop looking at her even as he nodded. "Yeah, tomorrow will be a full day. I'll have Kinsey text you when she gets in, and give you the address. Will I see you… I mean, will you be there when we get to my place, or will you just drop off whatever you buy for Greta? Which I'll reimburse you for, by the way."

"Whatever I get her can just be my welcome-to-Denver gift. And…I guess I did say I'd see her in Denver, but I don't know if it will be tomorrow."

Tomorrow, when *he* would get to see her—that was the way he'd put it at first, as if it wasn't about Greta at all.

Tomorrow, when Livi would get to see *him*—something she was thinking and trying not to.

"I guess it depends on how things go," she said. "When you get in. What I'm up to."

Whether or not the doctor rid her of her anxiety or confirmed it…

"But I'll try," she said. "For Greta's sake."

"Sure—for Greta's sake," he repeated.

Then he straightened and stepped back, opening the door wider for Livi to get in.

"Travel safe tomorrow," he said.

"You, too."

"And we'll take this show to Denver," he announced, sounding daunted, and making her laugh at him.

She started the engine and, taking his cue, Callan closed her door and turned back to the house.

Livi put her car into gear, but her eyes followed him, guiltily appreciating the sight.

There was just no denying that he was one of the finest-looking men she'd ever seen. Even from the back, where her gaze rode along for a while on that derriere-to-die-for.

But as he climbed the porch steps she reminded herself of all that was waiting for him inside that farmhouse. All that he had on his own plate.

A lot.

Too much.

That wildly hot man who had grown up dealing with more than any child should have had to, and was now determined to pay back what little help he'd been given.

What if she had to add to that burden? she asked herself as she tore her eyes off him and finally made the U-turn to drive away.

What if she told him he was going to be a father—how would he take it?

And why, even in the midst of all that she was fretting about, was a completely separate portion of her brain thinking once more about that Hawaiian kiss?

And yearning ever so slightly for him to do it again…

Chapter Five

Here we go, Callan thought as his private plane left the runway at a Montana airport, headed for Denver.

It was after four on Wednesday afternoon before they took off. Callan had been hoping to leave earlier, but it was tough to get the Tellers away. And hard on them to leave their home.

The last—and closest—of their friends and neighbors had begun to stream in to say goodbye at dawn, and the visits had gone on from there. Callan hadn't wanted to cut any of those goodbyes short. There was no love lost between himself and Northbridge or anyone in it, but for the Tellers it was a different story. They'd planned to live and die in the small town, surrounded by the people they'd shared the best and worst with for their entire lives.

So not until that stream had stopped had he texted his

pilot with a departure time, and finally loaded Maeve, John Sr. and Greta into the truck of the neighbor driving them to the airport.

It had been a long, silent drive during which Maeve—sitting across the truck's backseat with her leg braced on her husband's lap—had quietly cried. John Sr. had held her hand and patted her knee comfortingly, but his own jaw was clenched so tight that it seemed as if it might lock.

In the front seat, sitting between Callan and the driver, not even the chatty Greta had said a word. She'd just clutched her favorite doll and stared pensively ahead at the dashboard, not crying like her grandmother, but looking so sad it nearly broke Callan's heart.

He couldn't have felt worse for tearing three people from the only place any of them had ever called home. But he didn't know what comfort to give for a cut as deep as they were suffering, and he didn't know what else he could have done besides moving them all to Denver with him.

He'd assured them that he would get them back to Northbridge and the farm to visit often. But his business was in Denver and that's where he had to be. That's where he had to raise Greta. And while he'd offered to pay for continuous care and help for the Tellers to stay in Northbridge, they'd agreed that they wanted to be close to their granddaughter, and so had opted to go wherever she would be.

But it wasn't a good day for any of them, and as the flight got under way, Callan suggested a movie and started it for them.

Then he settled back and, for some reason, found himself instantly thinking that at the end of the dark tunnel that was today, at least there would be Livi Camden.

Kinsey would be there, too, he reminded himself. And that was good. He appreciated that—especially after having had to manage the Tellers without her today.

But still, it was Livi he was thinking of as the bright spot.

He tried to unseat her by thinking about Kinsey and Livi side by side. Because he recognized that the nurse was very attractive. If he was going to be unwillingly haunted by images of a woman, why Livi and not her?

No matter how hard he tried, however, it wasn't Kinsey who occupied his thoughts, it was Livi. The same way she'd been popping into his head almost constantly since they'd reconnected.

But why? Sure, at first maybe guilt for the way things had played out in Hawaii had caused it. But since they'd cleared the air about that? It was still happening and he couldn't figure it out.

He hadn't even thought this much about Elly, the woman he'd *married*. Of course, that had been part of the problem.

With all his energies focused on his business, he hadn't been there for Elly much. Instead, he'd delegated a lot of the "husband" responsibilities to his assistant. It had been up to Trent Baxter to pick out her anniversary presents, give her a lift when her car broke down, escort her to the society benefits Elly liked and Callan hated.

But somewhere during the course of that Trent had overstepped his bounds and taken Callan's place in bed with Elly, as well…

Lesson learned—marriage wasn't for him. And now, with the responsibility for Greta and the Tellers on his shoulders, he doubted he'd even have time for casual dating. So his preoccupation with Livi was a waste of time.

And yet he still couldn't get her off his mind.

What the hell was going on with him?

Maybe it was happening because when he was thinking about Livi he wasn't worrying about the change his life was taking. He wasn't fretting about how he was ever going to adapt to the whole family thing or meet everyone's needs. Every time he thought about *that* he felt as if he was rushing straight into another monumental failure like he'd had with Elly. Times three.

So maybe thinking about Livi was some kind of escape hatch.

After all, he'd met her the first time in a tropical paradise. So now, when he needed a breather, maybe his mind just made some sort of connection—Livi equaled a getaway. And Lord knew he needed that, if only in his thoughts.

His divorce had been finalized just four months ago. Two months later he'd lost the people he'd been closest to, the friends he'd depended on, for most of his life. Since then he'd been running himself ragged, going back and forth between Northbridge and Denver. But the hardest part was dealing with the Tellers and Greta.

He had his marriage to prove what a colossal failure he was when it came to emotional relationships with anyone other than Mandy and J.J.—who, he knew, had done most of the heavy lifting to keep their friendship going.

And now here he was, dealing with not one, not two, but three people who weren't Mandy and J.J., and the relationships and everything else that came with them.

He was up to his neck in it and definitely needed some relief. So somewhere in the course of things, he'd apparently connected rest and relaxation with Livi, and surely that was why he couldn't stop thinking about her. Why she seemed like the light at the end of the tunnel. That's all it was.

That was why last night, standing out in the fresh country air alone with her, talking, Callan had felt more relaxed than he had in two months. But he certainly wasn't looking for a repeat of their affair.

Sure, that night in Hawaii had been great.

Sure, he felt something good wash through him the minute he caught sight of her now.

Sure, he'd lost track of time, talking to her last evening. And his willful brain had even drifted into thoughts of kissing her under the Montana moonlight the way he'd kissed her under the Hawaiian moon.

But none of that made any difference.

A vacation fling was one thing, but with Livi stepping into Greta's life, he was going to have to be around her on a regular basis. If he wanted to be with her, it would have to be a real relationship—and he knew better than to try for that. He'd bombed out so thoroughly with Elly that he was in no state of mind to try again anytime soon. Or maybe ever. But certainly not when his divorce was only four months old. Not when he'd lost his own support team in Mandy and J.J. Not when he had the Tellers and Greta, who all needed what he was already afraid he might not be able to give—time and attention and thought.

And not when Livi was a Camden. Greta needed a woman to turn to, and Livi might be able to fill that role for now. But with time, Callan hoped to be able to find someone else to take over, both because he knew Mandy wouldn't want a Camden in her daughter's life, and because he wasn't sure himself if he could trust her. He knew that that was where some of his own issues overlapped and made things worse. After his experiences with Elly, he was finding it a struggle to consider trusting any woman again.

And when the any-woman was a Camden?

As far as he was concerned, no one could be less trustworthy than a Camden...

"You're awfully pale. Are you feeling okay?" Kinsey Madison asked.

Livi had arrived late Wednesday afternoon at Callan's condominium, located in a stately building behind Denver's Cherry Creek Shopping Center. Kinsey was already there and had shown her around the expansive four-bedroom, four-bath place. Then Kinsey had helped her arrange the dolls and stuffed animals she'd brought for Greta, after which Livi had offered to help make Maeve's accommodations more comfortable. They'd been hard at work when the nurse made her observation.

"I'm fine," Livi answered. "Long day, is all. You drove all the way from Northbridge today, you must be feeling a bit weary yourself."

"I stopped at my apartment and took a nap before coming over here, so I'm not doing too badly," Kinsey said.

Livi had gone straight from the airport to her gynecologist and then home, too. But napping hadn't been possible. Being told by her doctor that she was definitely pregnant hadn't made for a restful homecoming.

"You're sure you aren't coming down with something?" Kinsey persisted.

I'm coming down with something, all right—a baby in seven months.

And between now and then she would have to face her family with the news and let them know how it had happened.

She had no idea how she was ever going to do that.

And then there was Callan.

She didn't know what she was going to do about him, either.

But of course she couldn't say any of that, so she shook her head and said to the nurse, "I'm just tired."

Tired and spent from the hours she'd passed alternately crying and staring into space until it finally, genuinely sank in—she was going to have a baby.

Without Patrick.

But it was still a baby.

Her baby.

Something she'd wanted once upon a time; something she'd grieved losing the possibility of, along with grieving Patrick. But something that she would now get to have.

Livi wasn't happy. But she'd reached some sort of acceptance and had begun to feel a tiny ember of something that, given time, might turn into excitement.

As long as she didn't think about Callan.

Which was remarkably difficult when there was also some part of herself she didn't recognize that *kept* thinking about him. And not only in terms of the baby.

She kept thinking about talking to him the night before and how, like in Hawaii, time had flown by and she'd been in no hurry to have it end. She kept remembering so many tiny details of the way he looked, and how she'd gotten lost in studying them. She even kept hearing the sound of his deep voice in her head and feeling some kind of strange ripple every time she did.

Livi realized belatedly that Kinsey was still talking to her.

"Your family is big, isn't it? I mean, if what I've read in newspapers and magazines is true," she was saying.

"It is big—and getting bigger and bigger," Livi answered as they moved some furniture around.

"There's your grandmother, right?" Kinsey continued. "And ten kids who came from just her two sons?"

"You really have read about us," Livi said with a laugh. Under other conditions the nurse's questions might have seemed nosy. But in the little while since they'd met, Livi had come to like Kinsey, who she guessed to be near her age. So this just seemed more like the beginning of a friendship. Besides, Livi had grown up in the public eye as a Camden and was used to people knowing about her family.

She confirmed that yes, all ten of the Camden grandchildren had come from only two sons, Mitchum and Howard.

"And which of them was your father?"

"Mitchum."

Since it seemed as if Kinsey was making friendly overtures, Livi thought she should, too, so she said, "What about your family? Big? Small?"

"My mom just died."

"I'm so sorry," Livi murmured.

"Thanks," Kinsey responded, before going on. "I've lived in Denver since leaving home for college, but Mom was the reason I was in Northbridge. My three brothers and I grew up there—on a farm about the size of the

Tellers' place, and not far away—with Mom and our adopted father."

"Were your parents divorced?"

Kinsey didn't answer that immediately. For some reason she hesitated, then said, "No. Our father died when Mom was pregnant with me. She married Hugh Madison when I was two. He died a year ago. Mom stayed on the farm, but she didn't do well after that. I quit my job in Denver to take care of her when she started to really fail."

"How about your brothers? Did they help, too?"

"They're marines—all three of them overseas in Afghanistan. They couldn't get here. One of them—Declan—was injured the same day Mom died."

"Ohh…is he all right?"

"He'll survive, but he was pretty badly hurt. He's had two surgeries at the naval hospital there, but now he's being transferred to a hospital in Germany for a third operation that might include amputating his leg. Our oldest brother, Conor, is a doctor, and he's with Declan. Conor can't treat him because he's family, but he's overseeing things. So neither of them could get back for Mom's funeral. Declan's twin, Liam, was on a special mission and couldn't be reached at all. He didn't know Mom had died or that Declan had been hurt until a few days ago. So I've been on my own with…well, everything."

Kinsey sounded as if she'd faced her own overwhelming situation. Sympathizing, Livi was inclined to say she was sorry again, but wasn't sure it was called for.

So instead she said, "You went back to Northbridge to take care of you mother and her affairs, but ended up working with the Tellers?"

"Maeve fell the day after my mom's funeral. The doctor in Northbridge put Callan in touch with me to take care of her. It was a good fit because I could start there, and then come back here when they made the move."

But that seemed to be as much as Kinsey wanted to say about herself, because she returned to asking Livi about her family—her siblings and cousins, her grandmother and especially her father.

And since it kept the conversation away from her current troubles, Livi just let that happen and answered Kinsey's questions.

But as she did, she began to think about how nice Kinsey was, how warm and personable. And how pretty, too; she had coloring like Livi's own—dark hair, fair skin and blue eyes.

Livi began to think that if any of her brothers or male cousins were still single she would have told them about the home health care practitioner and offered to set one of them up on a date. But none of them were single anymore.

Callan was, though...

Had he noticed Kinsey? Livi wondered all of a sudden.

How could he not have? Circumstances put them together a lot. And Kinsey had plenty of charms to attract a healthy single guy.

But why did it bother her to think that surely he *had* noticed the pretty nurse? That he could even be attracted to her?

Was that why he was so eager to put Hawaii behind them? So he could feel free to start something up with Kinsey?

"Are you sure you're okay?" the nurse asked, sounding alarmed. "I thought you were pale before, but the color just disappeared from your face altogether."

"Really, I'm just tired," Livi repeated in a clipped tone.

But what if there was something going on between Kinsey and Callan? she asked herself.

It shouldn't affect her. It shouldn't matter to her. She should be glad for everyone involved. After all, Greta and the Tellers were already fond of the nurse and she was good to them. Callan clearly needed help. If he and Kinsey got together the whole lot of them could be one big happy family.

And Livi hated the idea so much she was tempted to take the decorative geode from the wooden plank coffee table they were about to move and throw it at Kinsey.

Perfectly nice Kinsey, who was doing nothing but being friendly to everyone, including her.

Perfectly nice Kinsey, who Livi had not seen Callan take any special interest in at all.

Perfectly nice Kinsey, who only seemed peripherally aware of Callan and even then only as her employer.

But still the thought of the two of them together was so horrible to Livi that she didn't know what to do now that she'd had it.

She was aware that what she was feeling was ridiculous. And she reminded herself that she'd had Patrick. Patrick was her one-and-only. He couldn't be replaced. Whatever went on in any other man's life didn't matter to her.

But *why* did she have to remind herself of that? She'd never had to before. It had always been so deeply ingrained in her that she never lost sight of it.

"Maybe I better sit down for just a minute," she muttered, wilting onto the sofa once they had the coffee table centered in front of it.

"I'll get you a glass of water," Kinsey said, leaving her alone.

Livi took a few deep breaths, trying to calm herself. Trying to clear her head. Trying to understand.

Maybe this was because of hormones?

The doctor had said she was flooded with them now. So many that they were already making enough changes in her body for the ob-gyn not to need a blood test to confirm the pregnancy. That had to be what was wrong with her. Why else would she be so freaked out by the thought of Callan with Kinsey?

The nurse returned with a glass of water and handed it to her. Livi thanked her, then blurted, "So I'll bet you'll be glad to see Callan when he gets here."

No! She hadn't really said that, had she?

Kinsey laughed slightly. "So he can move his own furniture?" she guessed.

Livi forced a laugh of her own, gratefully seizing the excuse Kinsey was giving her, because she felt like an idiot for what she'd said. "This stuff is massive," she added with a nod toward the pieces, which were large enough to fill the room and substantial for even the two of them to have to push across the hardwood flooring, since they were too heavy to lift.

"We're doing okay. If being without my brothers has taught me anything it's that women can do whatever they have to do without men."

Oh, God, I hope so... Livi thought.

She was going to have this baby on her own. And maybe that's what had caused that strange burst of jealousy? Maybe it was a biological thing, to want her baby's father to be free to take care of her and the child?

But even if she and Callan were having a baby, that didn't mean they were anything else to each other. Or that he couldn't or wouldn't or shouldn't go on to find his own one-and-only. She should even be hoping that he would. Eventually.

Maybe just not today.

And maybe not Kinsey.

Livi finished the glass of water and got to her feet as if she had renewed energy. "Okay, ready to go again," she announced.

But as she and Kinsey got back to work she started thinking of what single men she did know.

And who she might be able to fix the nurse up with in a hurry.

"I never turn down help cleaning," Callan said to Livi several hours later.

He'd arrived home with his three charges at a little after seven o'clock. Then he'd left the Tellers to Kinsey, Greta to Livi, and gone back out to pick up the dinner they'd all agreed on, while Livi and Kinsey got everyone shown around the condo and moved in to their respective rooms.

They'd all eaten when he'd returned with the food, then left the mess so that Callan and John Sr. could rearrange the furniture in the room the elder Tellers would occupy, while Kinsey got Maeve ready for bed and Livi urged Greta in that direction, too.

Greta had fallen asleep almost the minute her head hit the pillow, and once the Tellers' room was in order Callan had left Kinsey to deal with the elderly couple.

Slipping out of Greta's room, Livi had found him tackling the dining room and kitchen, and asked if he wanted another pair of hands.

But she wasn't just trying to be helpful.

From the moment Callan had gotten there she'd been

watching him and Kinsey. Hating herself for it. Not understanding why she was so driven to do it, but doing it, anyway.

She hadn't seen a single indication that there was anything going on between them, but something in her wouldn't let her leave until she knew Kinsey was gone, too.

So she'd offered to help Callan clean up.

"A Camden doing the dishes—is this a first?" he asked jokingly.

"It is a first," she said teasingly. "As a Camden I've always had a whole staff to do everything for me—put the toothpaste on my toothbrush, cut my food, hold the cup with my morning coffee for me to sip out of, dab the corners of my mouth after every bite I'm fed by my feeder…"

He laughed. "I know it isn't like that, but you *are* a Camden."

"Clearly you've never met my grandmother. She was a farm girl from Northbridge—get her started and you hear stories about slopping pigs and milking cows and what it really means to get your hands dirty. And since she raised me—along with my five brothers and sisters and four cousins—from the time I was six years old, I can promise you that I have done more dishes than you've probably seen in your lifetime."

"That's a *lot* of brothers and sisters and cousins. Your grandmother raised you all after the plane crash?" he asked as they stacked take-out containers, gathered used napkins, plates, silverware and glasses. "I remember hearing about the crash when it happened, but I was just a kid myself. I never thought about there being kids left behind until now."

"Well, there were. A full ten of us. I'm just grateful we still had my grandmother—plus my great-grandfather, H. J. Camden. He's the one who started the whole Camden enterprise. The two of them had to stay home at the last minute because H.J. had hurt his back. They ended up being the only two left to take care of us."

"Or they would have been lost, too," Callan said with some astonishment. "It's weird. Until now I've only been on the other side of this. I have to admit, I wasn't heart-broken that the people who had stolen Mandy's dad's business didn't end up living long and prosperous lives themselves."

Livi didn't know what to say to that.

"Sorry, that was…" Callan paused, then said, "I have some mixed feelings going on here. On the one hand you're Livi. From Hawaii. And when that's all you are… well, I can't say I hate being around you."

That sounded like an understatement. Did it mean that he *liked* being with her?

"On the other hand," he continued, "you're a Camden. And one of my best friends hated Camdens so much I wouldn't have trusted her to be in the same room with one. So when that part comes up…I guess I go into Mandy-mode and…well, I'm sorry if I say something I shouldn't."

Livi nodded, distracted by his inadvertent admission that he liked being with her.

Then he seemed to make an effort to separate her from her family name, and said, "So tell me about being raised by your grandmother. Ten of you, huh?"

"Ten kids, yeah," she confirmed. "But only eight births, because I'm a triplet with my brother Lang and my sister, Lindie."

"I've never met a triplet before."

"You don't run into too many of us. Lang and Lindie and I, and our cousin Jani, are the youngest of the family—Jani is the same age we are."

"So she was six when the plane crash happened, too."

"Right. GiGi—that's what we call our grandmother—took over after that and raised us all. With some help from H.J., who had to come out of retirement at eighty-eight to run Camden Inc., and with Margaret and Louie Haliburton, who started out as staff but became just like family."

"They were the ones who put the toothpaste on your toothbrush?" Callan teased.

Livi laughed and appreciated that he'd lightened the tone. "I think they might have, actually. Once or twice when I was little. But the Camden name and coffers didn't mean a thing to GiGi. She raised us the way she'd been raised."

"You had pigs to slop and cows to milk?"

"No, but every one of us had chores, from the moment we went to live with GiGi until the day any one of us moved out—and even on vacations home from college. We all still pitch in there when something needs to be done."

"But you started doing chores when you were six?"

"I did. I learned to make my own bed, pick up after myself, and we all got together in the kitchen every single weeknight to lend a hand making dinner and then cleaning up."

"So *you* were the staff?" he joked again.

"We were just one big family. We worked together and played together and we're still a pretty tight-knit group."

"And it sounds like you like that."

"I did and do. There's always been company and support and help when any one of us needs it…" Things she knew she was going to need again now, facing pregnancy and single parenthood. Things she was counting on. "We still do what GiGi started all those years ago—we have movie nights at her house, dinner every Sunday. We share the responsibilities and run Camden Incorporated equally and keep up with each other's lives and babysit for one another and whatever."

"So basically your grandmother is an expert at doing the whole family thing."

"Well, yeah…" Livi said, hearing in his voice that the idea seemed foreign to him.

"And now that I'm doing what she did, taking over for Mandy and J.J., that puts me in her position? Does that mean I should do that kind of thing?" he asked, as if this was news to him.

"Should you assign chores so Greta learns responsibility? Cook dinner yourself every night and make sure the whole family is together for Sunday dinner every week? Should you have movie nights and arrange fun stuff for everyone to do together? I suppose you have to make it work for you and the Tellers and Greta, so there might be variations of all that, but sure. Were you not thinking about being Greta's family now? Because you are… Along with the Tellers, of course, but they won't be around forever. And you aren't just loaning rooms out in your house."

"I guess I didn't really think about any of that," he admitted, frowning as they began to take things from the formal dining room into Callan's ultracontemporary kitchen.

Neither of them said anything as they made a few trips

to clear the dining room. Livi had the impression that he was contemplating what seemed to have been a revelation to him. She left him to it as she packaged leftovers and he rinsed plates and put them in the dishwasher.

They'd just about finished when Kinsey came in to say that Maeve and John Sr. were in bed for the night and she was leaving, that she would be back the next morning.

Livi thought she should say good-night, too, and walk out with the nurse. But the kitchen wasn't completely clean. The dining room table needed to be washed off. And she *had* volunteered to help...

Oh, who was she kidding? She just wasn't eager to have her time there end yet.

Callan said only a perfunctory good-night to the nurse, without casting a glance in her direction, as he loaded the dishwasher.

He didn't seem to hear Kinsey say in a more casual, genial voice to Livi, "Get some rest tonight."

"You, too," Livi countered.

Then Kinsey said a general "See you all tomorrow" that only Livi answered, and left.

When she had, Callan's attention was solely on Livi again.

"Didn't you sleep well last night?" he asked.

No, she hadn't slept well. Not with that doctor's appointment this morning on her mind. But she didn't want to mention that, so she said, "I was up early to leave Northbridge—the same way Kinsey was. We were commiserating before you got here." It was Livi's turn to pause before she said, "She's nice..."

Callan shrugged. "Kinsey? Yeah, she is," he agreed vaguely. "I haven't had a whole lot of interaction with her—she keeps me updated, but she's just sort of… around, doing her job. But yeah, she's nice enough."

"She's pretty, too," Livi said, confused by why she had such a need to push this with him. But she did. "Is she single? I've never heard her mention anyone."

"Maeve says she is—I think it was some kind of hint that I should take a look or something." More ambiguity.

"But you didn't?"

"Nah," he said, as if he couldn't give it a second thought.

And yet Livi was still compelled to test. "I was thinking that I might fix her up. I know a few single men she might like…"

"Just don't get her all wrapped up in some new romance until I can spare her around here."

The fact that he was so focused on Kinsey's work—and nothing else about the pretty nurse—made Livi feel worlds better as she went into the dining room to wipe down the table.

When she returned to the kitchen, Callan had that finished, too, and after rinsing the sponge she'd used and handing it to him to put away, it occurred to her that there was nothing more holding her there.

"I should probably get going, too," she said.

"There's no rush…"

Because he wanted her to stay or because he was being polite?

It didn't matter, she told herself. She'd come to welcome Greta, she'd pitched in out of good manners and now it was time to go.

Like it or not…

"It's been a long day," she replied, repeating what she'd said earlier to Kinsey. "For you, too."

"I'm fine," he insisted.

So maybe he wasn't just being polite?

It was satisfying to think that he wanted her to stay—and tempting, too—but she thought better of it and didn't give in to the inclination to.

"I really should get going."

"I'll walk you down to your car then," he said. "The parking garage is pretty secure, but I'm still not crazy about the idea of a woman down there alone at night."

Livi didn't point out that he'd just let Kinsey leave alone, because she didn't want to admit to herself that she didn't hate the prospect of him escorting her to her car.

And she also didn't want to encourage him to start being more attentive to Kinsey.

So she just picked up her purse and put on her jacket.

Callan opened the door for her and they stepped across the hall to the elevator that brought them down to the basement level, where she'd been directed to park.

"The dolls and stuffed animals were a big hit. Thanks for doing that for Greta," Callan said along the way.

"I'm just glad she liked them all. I wasn't sure what she might already have, so I went into the toy department in our store on Colorado Boulevard and asked for the newest arrivals that sales figures indicate are trending for her age group."

"You had a plan," he said with a laugh. Livi flushed as she realized after the fact that her explanation was more detailed than it needed to be.

It was just that being alone with him, standing so close in the elevator, made her even more aware of him. How substantially built he was. How much she liked the cologne he wore.

They reached her car, but tonight Callan stopped short of going to her door. Instead he hitched a hip onto her rear fender and crossed his forearms over the thick thigh he raised.

Livi obliged him and came to a stop, too, facing him. And trying to ignore the fact that even dressed in casual navy blue twill slacks and a white polo shirt, he was something to see. Especially with that stubble shadowing his bad-boy good looks.

"So you're taking Greta shopping for things to redecorate her room tomorrow?" he said then.

Ah, so that was what he wanted to talk about. He was probably having misgivings about it again.

"If that's okay," Livi answered. "I know it was Maeve's suggestion at dinner, and you didn't say much. But I wasn't sure how long I'd be in Northbridge, so I took all this week off and I'm free…"

"I'd like to be there, but I've been gone for twelve days this time, to close up the farm and get everybody ready for this move. I have to go into work."

"And your favorite thing to do is shop for stuff to redecorate a room, and you don't want it done without you?"

He laughed again. "Actually, to me, that kind of shopping is punishment enough for a capital crime—I *hate* it. But…"

"You want to keep an eye on me when I'm with Greta in case I'm an evil Camden and not on the up-and-up," Livi said, paraphrasing his warning that first day at the farm and also recalling his reservations when they'd talked about this before.

He grinned sheepishly and confessed, "Something like that."

"So do you not want us to go tomorrow?"

He took a moment to think about it, not looking at her. Then he drew a deep breath and sighed. "Greta was really excited about it," he admitted. "She hardly said five words all day long, but when Maeve came up with that…" His eyebrows arched as if in concession.

"She's big enough for you to question when we get back, you know," Livi suggested. "You can keep tabs on things that way to monitor me."

She didn't know what about that made him flash a devilish little smile, before he said, "I s'pose. You've kind of got me over a barrel, having Maeve in your corner."

"I won't do it if you're uncomfortable with it," Livi said. "I'll even take the blame—I can call Greta in the morning and say something came up and I can't make it."

"That would make you the bad guy instead of me," he said, as if there was some appeal in that. But then he shook his head. "No, that would disappoint Greta. And I want her room to be what she wants. But I'm paying this time. Whatever she picks out, have the salesperson call me and I'll give my credit card number for it."

It was Livi's turn to laugh, because he'd said that as if it somehow justified him agreeing to let Greta be alone with her. "If that makes you feel better. And I swear I'll try not to corrupt her while we're picking out dust ruffles."

"I don't know what a dust ruffle is, but thanks," he said facetiously. He shook his head again. "I told you, this is all pretty mixed up for me."

Livi nodded. "I get it—it'll just take some time for you to see that I really only want to make up for what was done years ago."

"So you aren't a Camden Trojan horse."

"What exactly would I be infiltrating?" she challenged, a part of her realizing how much she liked these teasing exchanges.

"I don't know. I only know how Mandy felt about Camdens, and I'm trying to do right by her."

"I respect that," Livi admitted. "You're just being a good friend and looking out for her daughter."

And it was something about him and his character that she noted herself. Admiring it in him even if it did make him suspicious of her.

He was studying her face as if to reassure himself. Or maybe to resolve those two elements that he found at odds—her being whatever it was he'd thought of her in Hawaii with the fact that she was a Camden.

Then he pushed off her fender and stood in front of her. "It's also tough," he confided, "because Camden or not, you're a big help to me. And I need it all the way around. At least, while I'm trying to figure this whole thing out, Greta doesn't have to suffer for my incompetence as her guardian."

"So think of it as that—help to you that Greta benefits from."

"That sounded a little Trojan horsey—like you're trying to suck me in so I lower my guard," he said with one eyebrow arched.

But his voice was more playful than venomous. And the expression on his handsome face changed to something more intimate.

Then he reached a hand to her upper arm, squeezing it affectionately, as if that was a perfectly natural thing between them. "Anyway, thanks for what you did today and for sticking around tonight. Like I said, it put Greta in a better mood, and I think the Tellers were happy to see you, too." He paused a beat, squeezed her arm a second time, and added, "And I can't say I was *un*happy to see you…"

She liked hearing that more than she wanted to.

Then, when she wasn't expecting it at all, he leaned forward and kissed her forehead.

Livi froze, taken by surprise and knocked off balance by that contact.

But it was over the next moment when he let go of her arm to step back.

Nodding toward the driver's side of her car, he said, "Go on home and get some sleep."

Livi swallowed with some difficulty and could barely find her voice to say good-night before she did as he'd instructed.

But after an entire day of muddled emotions, as she drove home she felt even more confusion.

In her entire life she had never seen herself with anyone but Patrick.

In Hawaii she'd been outside of herself. But here she was now, with her feet firmly planted on home turf.

And while she wasn't actually seeing herself with Callan, something did seem to be happening.

Something she didn't understand, that had never happened before.

Something that left her arm still tingling where Callan had touched her.

Something that left her hungering for more than that platonic forehead kiss.

And thinking—for the first time, here and now, on home turf—that maybe Patrick *wasn't* the only man she could be with...

Chapter Six

"Good, you're still here! But everybody else—"

"Sound asleep. Kinsey left a few minutes ago, and I was just about to," Livi told Callan when he came in on Friday night. He'd caught her in the middle of putting on her short, black leather jacket over the white mock-turtleneck T-shirt topping her jeans and boots.

"Damn, I did it again?" he said.

Livi assumed he meant that he'd come home from work for the second day in a row too late for any of his charges to so much as set eyes on him. And according to Greta, he left for work before they woke in the morning, so none of them had seen him since Wednesday night.

Neither had Livi—something she was more aware of than she wanted to be.

On Thursday she'd taken Greta shopping, making sporadic contact with Callan along the way through texts, and thinking that she would see him that evening. Looking forward to seeing him, in spite of herself.

But a little before six he'd texted that he was held up and wouldn't be home for dinner. He'd asked if she could pick something up. So Livi and Greta had ordered takeout from an Italian bistro next to the mall and brought it home for everyone. Callan still hadn't shown up when Livi had put Greta to bed and Kinsey had done the same with Maeve.

This morning, Livi, Greta, Kinsey and John Sr., supervised by Maeve in her wheelchair, had started turning Greta's room into a nine-year-old girl's dream, a project that took them into the evening.

Still no sign of Callan.

And because during the last two days Greta's highs had been sprinkled with some very low lows, Livi hadn't wanted to just leave her. So she'd suggested the five of them have a pizza-and-movie night.

Which was what they'd done.

But even though Greta had stayed up past her bedtime, eager to show Callan all they'd done to her room, by ten o'clock Maeve insisted that her granddaughter get to bed, and the elder Tellers had followed suit.

Since the pizza and movie had been Livi's idea, along with popcorn, she'd stayed to clean up, sending Kinsey home once the nurse had finished getting Maeve situated for the night.

And even though Livi told herself she wasn't consciously stalling in hopes of seeing Callan, she knew she sort of was. But she'd run out of excuses to stay, and so she was about to leave when he came in.

"What time is it?" he asked, keeping his voice low as he took off his tan suit coat and striped tie.

"Not quite eleven," she informed him, going on to explain about the movie and cleanup and Greta trying to wait for him, certainly not letting him know that she had been, too. And trying hard not to feast on the sight of him as if she were starving for it.

"I brought doughnuts..." he said, as if they were consolation, raising the bakery box he was carrying.

"They can eat them for breakfast?" Livi proposed.

He nodded, but said, "I blew it, huh?"

She merely raised her eyebrows at him to confirm it.

"Can you hang around a little bit and bring me up to date? I know it's late, but..." He raised the box again and repeated temptingly, "I have doughnuts. And tonight is the first night the fire pits were lit in the courtyard downstairs. It's still a nice night. We could take the doughnuts down there and talk..."

It was late and pregnancy was sapping Livi's energy.

But it *was* Friday night, and there was nowhere she needed to be in the morning. Plus there were a few things she thought he should be updated on. Besides, there was nothing and no one waiting for her at home—just an empty house.

"I'm weak when it comes to doughnuts," she said.

He grinned as if she'd granted him something deeply important. "Give me five minutes to change clothes and I'll be right back," he said, handing her the pastry box.

This isn't because I feel any kind of attraction to him, she told herself while he was gone.

It couldn't be.

If she was genuinely attracted to him it would be another complication in an already overly complex situation. She needed to be able to think clearly in order to make sure she made the right choices now. Much, much better choices than she'd made in Hawaii.

So while she knew she needed to get to know Callan, what she didn't need was any kind of emotions clouding the situation.

Yet when he walked back into the entry a few minutes later, dressed in jeans that fitted him like an old friend and a gray hoodie that had somehow mussed his hair into looking even better than it had, coupled with that sexy stubble on his jaw Livi couldn't help appreciating the whole picture. Which made it difficult to go on believing that she wasn't attracted to him.

But still, she tried.

"Okay, let's go," he said, taking the doughnut box back and opening the door for her to step out ahead of him.

"You've been at work all this time?" she asked as they rode the elevator to the first floor.

"Before dawn yesterday until after midnight last night, and then in again before dawn today. We're launching new operating system software in another month and I've been gone to Northbridge so much that we're behind schedule. My people have been working overtime to make up for me not being there. Tempers are short and disputes had to be dealt with. And there were meetings I've been putting off, on top of work I'm behind on..." He stopped short. "You run a big business—you know how it is."

"I share responsibilities with nine other people, so the weight of everything doesn't fall on any one of us... So, no, we don't get as swamped as that."

"Lucky you," he said, as he guided her through the lobby and out a back door into a courtyard that made Livi feel as if she'd stepped into a forest retreat.

A flat, grassy meadow-like area was enclosed in moss-covered rocks and evergreen trees that blocked out any view or sounds of the city, and instead made it seem as if they were in the mountains.

But the setting was luxurious, too, with lushly cushioned outdoor furniture surrounding several fire pits. They were all lit, giving off enough heat to chase away any chill.

"Great—we have it all to ourselves," Callan said, motioning to the grouping not far from the door.

Each fire pit was centered amid four seats larger than easy chairs, providing more than enough room for one. Livi sat where he directed and he joined her, keeping it cozy. Especially when he rested his arm on top of the wrought-iron frame behind her. He wasn't touching her in any way, but it *was* cozy.

And nice.

Though again, she tried not to register that.

He opened the doughnut box and held it out to her.

There was a chocolate-glazed chocolate one with chocolate sprinkles; Livi didn't have to think twice.

"You're a chocolate girl," he observed.

"Through and through," she confessed, as he picked a plain glazed and set the box on the small table beside their chair.

"These will be even better dunked in coffee tomorrow morning," he said, just before they both took a bite.

Her mornings hadn't included coffee for a few weeks because the smell of it made her sicker. And anyway, she was watching her caffeine intake now that she knew she was pregnant.

But that wasn't a comment she was going to make,

so she just took another bite of her doughnut, enjoying it tonight while she could.

"So what's been going on?" he asked.

Livi filled him in on the time since he'd last been with her or anyone else in his household, then said, "Greta has had a few rough patches. When we were shopping there were a couple of times when she mentioned her mom— like she forgot for a minute that Mandy was gone. Twice she said she liked something but didn't know if her mom would, then she caught herself and got really quiet. At home she kept asking Maeve if her parents would have liked her choices—as if she was hoping Maeve could channel some approval. And she kind of disappeared into her room last night, and when I found her she was crying."

Callan sobered and frowned. "Is that normal?"

"I talked to her about what it was like for me when I lost my parents, when I had to move away from my house to live somewhere else. That brought up a lot of questions about if I thought or felt this or that, as if she's been worrying that she might be doing it wrong. I told her I'd thought and felt the same things, and it seemed like she got a little happier."

"So she's going through what you went through and it *is* normal?"

"I think so."

"But it was a tough couple of days that I wasn't around for."

"It has been tough," Livi confirmed, without condemning him. "This is even more upheaval for her than I went through. I went from my home to my grandmother's house, somewhere I was familiar with. It doesn't seem as if you and Greta are as close as I was to GiGi…"

"I'm pretty busy all the time," he admitted.

"For Greta, this is all new and unfamiliar," Livi continued. "Your place is beautiful, but it isn't what she's used to and she's worrying about what she should use, what she can and can't touch, where she can and can't go in the condo. And the same goes for the Tellers, I think. Maeve keeps fretting about things being too nice to use, not wanting to risk damaging this or that. She tells John Sr. to be careful constantly. Plus, for John Sr.—"

"I'm in trouble all the way around, huh?"

Livi didn't want to scold Callan, but he needed to know what was going on. "You have to take into consideration how big a change this is for all of them. I think they need you around reassuring them that it's their home now, too. Or setting some sort of parameters if there are things you *don't* want them to do."

"They can do whatever they want," he said, as if he genuinely wasn't concerned.

"But they need to be made to feel welcome and at home. By you—because, after all, it's your place. But you've kind of disappeared on them. Maeve keeps worrying, and John Sr. is chafing at things—"

"The old man *chafes* at everything. Especially when it comes to me."

Any mention of the elder male Teller always seemed to rub Callan the wrong way, and vice versa. Livi ignored his comment. "But I think he's feeling kind of stranded. Maeve is incapacitated and not up to anything but resting, but John Sr. isn't. I mean, I can see where he couldn't handle all the farm work on his own anymore, or provide all the nursing of Maeve needs, but he's said more than once in these last two days that if he was home he could get in his truck and go into town to get—"

"His sunflower seeds and jerky and beer!" Callan said with a grimace. "I forgot. He was going to bring his own supply and I told him I'd stock them as soon as we got here, and I didn't."

Livi didn't mention that she knew that because the elderly man had complained about it. "I did a grocery run this morning and got what he wanted. But I think it's more than that. I think he needs a car—or truck—so whenever he feels like it he can get out for a while on his own. He's feeling kind of penned in…"

"Sure, but he was in Northbridge before, not Cherry Creek, where there's traffic. You know driving around here is a lot different than the open country roads he's used to."

"You could take him out, show him some back ways to get around and how to avoid traffic so he could at least go to the grocery store or the mall or whatever. Enough so he has some independence left. He's a proud old guy and—"

"And you're saying that I've cut him off at the knees. But you know, the Tellers aren't as young as your parents or mine would have been if they were still alive," he argued.

"I know. Maeve told me how John Jr. was a surprise late-in-life baby, that she was forty-five when she had him. But their age is all the more reason why they need some independence. I can tell you from the way things are with my grandmother that even basically healthy people that age end up with a lot of back and forth to doctors and pharmacies just for maintenance. Right now Kinsey is taking care of all the meds and monitoring for both Maeve and John Sr., but when she's gone, they'll need to get in to a doctor's office and a pharmacy more than you can imagine. John Sr. can take them around for a few more years if you just get him comfortable driving in the city. In the long run that's to your benefit, too."

"True…" Callan said thoughtfully.

"Kinsey examined him, gave him reflex and vision tests. She said he's fine on that count," Livi added, to convince him.

"Maybe he could even take Greta back and forth to school," Callan mused.

It was something else Livi had planned to use to build her case. But now that it had occurred to him on his own she was a little afraid he might go too far. Yes, the Tellers could help out shuttling Greta back and forth, but as her guardian, Callan should really take on some of those responsibilities himself.

So she said, "But even though John Sr. can pitch in a little, it would still be good if you kept to some kind of schedule where they all could expect to see you every day. Just leaving them wondering if you'll be around or not—"

"Is bad," he said, as if it was a complaint he'd heard before. "I know I have to pay more attention to what's going on at home. I'm just used to staying at work until the work is done, no matter how long that takes. I grab something to eat when I get hungry, not because it's any particular time of day. And—" his tone turned guilty "—I barely remember there's anyone at home, waiting. And I know that's lousy for whoever *is* at home. But at least I haven't had my assistant filling in." Callan sounded proud of himself for a moment, then frowned and added, "Although I guess that's pretty much what you and Kinsey have been doing…"

He released a sigh of self-disgust and said, "I really haven't learned my lesson."

"You took on responsibility for another elderly couple and a nine-year-old girl once before and should have learned something from it?" Livi joked.

"No, but I *did* neglect my wife right into the arms of my assistant."

Livi wasn't quite sure what to say to that. It did make her curious, though.

"I have a history of dropping the ball when it comes to relationships," Callan explained.

After seeing what had gone on for the last two days, Livi didn't find that a surprise.

He chuckled mirthlessly and added, "Actually, that dates all the way back to the sixth grade, when Mandy had a crush on me."

"Not on John Jr.?"

"Nope, that didn't happen until we were older. In fact, I was so oblivious that I didn't even know she'd ever felt that way about me until she told me about it years later. We all laughed about it because it had just been a kid thing. But after that I sometimes had the feeling that I was on the outside looking in at what I might have had."

"Did you have those kinds of feelings for Mandy?" Livi asked.

"No, I never saw her as anything but a friend. But you know, it's the what-if—what if I'd gone through that door instead of walking right past it."

"Greta would have been yours," Livi said, testing for his reaction.

But he only laughed. "I'm sure I would have screwed things up long before that—I have with every other woman. Mandy was always sending me on blind dates, trying to find me someone. But even when I liked the person, eventually the way I work got in the way."

"So it's common for you to work as hard and long as you have the last two days?"

"The past few days have been extreme, since I had a lot of catching up to do, and the product launch is around the corner. But we have our share of crises and they usually mean I end up chained to my desk. In any case, Mandy said I was bad about letting anybody get too close, that I used my job to make sure they didn't."

"But you did get married," Livi reminded him. "Was that from one of Mandy's setups?"

"Actually, no. I married my secretary."

Livi laughed. "A relationship you could *combine* with work?"

He laughed, too. "At first, I guess. Mostly it was a relationship that got scheduled in when I wasn't really looking."

"How does that happen?"

"Elly was my first secretary when CT Software took off. And, don't get me wrong, she was cute and smart and I was aware of it—I'm not blind. But mostly she was just around. If I worked, she worked. I didn't ask that of her, but she said that was her job. And it was nice having her there whenever I needed something—dinner ordered in at eleven at night, paperwork when I remembered it at four in the morning. I thought it was just loyalty, but—"

"It was a way to spend time with you." Sort of what Livi was doing, sitting in that courtyard with him as the clock ticked toward midnight.

"Right. Things got more and more chummy and then flirty. Elly started to make comments about how I owed her a night on the town for all the nights she'd worked, and she just sort of eventually scheduled herself in."

"Because who better to know when you *would* have time to get away from work."

"Yep."

"And by the time you got to paying her back for all those long work nights, you must have been fairly close. *From* all of those long work nights."

"Also yep. We were married the year after Greta was born."

It didn't sound very romantic, but Livi didn't say that. "So, you got married eight years ago? Did Elly stay your secretary?"

"For about three years. But then we bought some land to build a house on and she decided she wanted to do everything herself so the place would be exactly right. She thought that should be her full-time job. And it wasn't as if we needed the money, so she quit."

"While you kept on working the way you had?"

"Uh…yeah," he admitted reluctantly. "But for a while she didn't complain *too* much."

"She knew better than anyone how you were about your job."

"Right. And she was swamped herself with designing the house and overseeing the building and then decorating it."

"And did you have a new secretary?" Livi asked leadingly, hoping this story didn't end with him having an affair. She wanted to think he wasn't that kind of man.

"I did. The same one I have now. Rose, who's old enough to be my mother, is devoted to her husband and works strictly from nine to five. But along the way I also gained an assistant…" Callan finished that in an ominous tone. "A man named Trent Baxter, because Elly didn't want it to be a woman."

That wasn't difficult to understand. Especially not for Livi as she sat there watching him and thinking that she couldn't imagine any woman not being a little awe-struck by those good looks.

"How long was your wife occupied with building and decorating the new house?" she asked.

"Altogether? Almost three years. We moved in on our sixth anniversary—a day I remember too well, because on top of the move and the anniversary, we had a world-class fight."

"Seems like you should have been celebrating."

Looking embarrassed, he admitted, "I was at work for most of that day and it was my assistant filling in for me, overseeing the move. During the fight Elly said that I didn't have a mistress on the side, I had a wife on the side, and she called my assistant her 'proxy husband.'"

Livi flinched for him. "And how exactly was he your proxy?"

"Turned out, in all ways," Callan said under his breath. Then, more openly, he went on. "Besides being there for the move that day, Trent had taken on the job of buying my gifts for Elly, for birthdays and Christmas and all anniversaries and holidays and special occasions. Actually, too many times I didn't even give them to her—Trent ended up delivering them while I stayed working."

"Which you do a lot."

He nodded. "Trent took my place at social functions so Elly didn't have to go alone. I even sent him with medicine and chicken soup when she got sick, and to give her a lift when she had car trouble."

Livi could tell that he knew those were mistakes. "Did

you stop having your assistant be your proxy after the fight?"

"I'd like to say yes…"

"But you can't."

Apparently he couldn't. Instead he said, "Then Elly got pregnant unexpectedly, a little over a year ago."

His tone was more ominous still.

"I was happier about it than I expected to be," he said sadly.

"You didn't want kids before that?"

"I wasn't against the idea. But I was busy and…" He paused. "I know this will sound lazy or selfish or something, but it seemed like a wife was enough to keep up with."

"Even though it was really your assistant who was keeping up with her?"

"Yeah," he admitted ruefully. "But once I thought there was going to be a kid, I thought, okay, great, we'll have a family. Maybe we'll be like Mandy and J.J., after all. And I actually started to get kind of excited about it."

"So you didn't think your marriage was like your friends' marriage without kids?"

"It wasn't," he said categorically. "Not that I didn't love Elly. I did. And even though she sort of manipulated us into a relationship, I like to think that she loved me, too, that that's *why* she scheduled herself into my life. But did we have what Mandy and J.J. had? I can't explain why, but…we didn't. There was just something…I don't know…more superficial about the way we were together. I thought maybe it was just because Mandy and J.J. had history—hell, they had history even before they started dating. I thought maybe Elly and I just needed to put in more years together…"

"And that a baby would bring you closer?"

He shrugged. "I guessed that if we had a family, we'd seem more like a family—if that makes any sense. Coming from what I came from, it wasn't like I had a role model for being a husband and father. Yes, I lived with the Tellers for a year, but John Sr. never opened up to me, and there's only so much you can pick up by watching. I understood Mandy and J.J.'s relationship better, and what they had was great. I thought getting married would give me the same thing. But once I was in it, it didn't. Only I couldn't tell you what was lacking. Just that something was."

"And you think it was all you?" Livi guessed.

"I think I dropped the ball big-time and that if I had handled things differently, Elly would never have done what she did."

"Which was what?" Livi asked, admiring that he took responsibility for his own actions, but still wanting to know what part his wife had played.

"About six months into the pregnancy I got home one night to find Trent there waiting for me *with* Elly. So they could tell me together that they were pretty sure the baby was his and they wanted to get married. That *they* wanted to be a family."

Hearing the note of lingering shock in Callan's voice, Livi felt her heart go out to him. "Ouch," she said.

"Yeah. Believe it or not, it hit me hard. I never saw it coming—which I suppose makes me about the most oblivious person on earth after she'd already told me he was her 'proxy husband.'"

"And *was* the baby his?" Livi asked carefully.

"Yes—DNA tests proved it."

"A second punch," she sympathized.

"The whole thing was a jolt," Callan agreed with some sadness in his voice. "And, yes, it was rotten of Elly and Trent to hook up behind my back. But I'd handed them the opportunity on a platter—I neglected Elly. I neglected the relationship. I sent someone else in to do what I should have been doing."

He really was determined to take the blame. Livi could see that nothing she said would change his mind, so she opted for a different take.

"Okay, but now you have a chance to mend your wanton ways," she pointed out with some levity, trying to find something positive that might help with his current situation.

He smiled at her. "Was this a roundabout way of getting me to admit that I need to make it home for dinner every night?"

"Actually, I believe I sort of started out saying that," Livi stated.

"So I'm a slow learner, too?" he joked.

"Apparently not when it comes to computers, but maybe a little when it comes to people..."

"Okay, no denying it. If I promise to try harder would that make you feel better?"

"It would."

He smiled again and bowed slightly "Okay. I will try harder to remember there are people at home waiting for me, and to get there at regular intervals."

Livi laughed. "Well, it takes a little more than that, but that's a beginning, anyway."

"Lesson one. But you'd better leave it at that for now. You don't want to overwhelm a slow learner with too much at once."

"True. I think, seeing what I'm working with, patience is probably what it takes," she agreed, giving him a hard time.

He seemed to enjoy their back-and-forth, though, because the tension visible in his striking features when he'd been talking about his past was now gone. It was replaced by a little sparkle in those dark eyes that was not coming from the fire.

"Are you going to be around for any of the dinners I'm supposed to make sure I come home to?" he asked, with something else in his voice. Something enticing.

"I guess if I'm invited I might be," she said, more flirtatiously than she intended.

"How about I give you a blanket invitation here and now?"

"Forgetting that I'm a Camden and you aren't sure I should be around at all?" she challenged.

He grinned full-out then, drawing crinkles at the corners of his eyes. "Oh, yeah, I did forget about that. Again."

Maybe because he was looking into her eyes the same way he had two months ago in Hawaii, when they'd been just Livi and Callan.

And there on that comfy chair under the stars, bathed in the golden glow of the fire burning nearby, it felt as if they were again.

Callan's hand came from the back of the chair to her nape, so softly she barely felt it.

His eyes were still searching hers. And maybe it was due to the fact that it was so late and she was weary, or maybe it was being outdoors with him again, in the night air, but Livi didn't fight the feeling that took them back two months.

Instead, when he closed the distance between them,

she didn't draw away. She stayed where she was, letting him kiss her.

Not on the forehead tonight, however.

No, tonight he kissed her on the mouth, his lips warm and talented.

And without thinking about it, she found herself kissing him back, basking in sweetness that had a titillating bit of sensuality to it.

Then it was over and Callan was the one to draw away, taking a deep breath. "Yeah, just plain Livi tonight," he mused. "Without being plain at all... Could *you* fix *that*?" he teased.

Coming to her senses, Livi still couldn't help smiling at him. "You want me to wear a bag over my head?"

He grinned yet again. "No, I'd miss the sight of you. Even if it would make things easier on me."

She had to admit that it was nice to receive a little flattery. But she knew better than to let it go too far, so she took her own turn at a deep breath and stood up.

"It's late," she said. "And do you remember that tomorrow Greta is supposed to visit her new school?"

She could tell he hadn't. But he didn't own up to it. Instead he covered, saying, "I do seem to recall something about that. Even though it's Saturday, there's some kind of event, so the school will be open and the principal will be there. He'll have some free time on his hands and thought that would be a good opportunity to give her the tour."

"Right."

"And let me guess—Greta wants you there?" Callan said.

"But you need to be there, too," Livi warned.

He laughed, standing along with her and picking up

the bakery box with the remainder of the doughnuts. "You don't trust me to know that without prompting?" he challenged, as they headed back inside.

"After your disappearing act the last couple of days?"

"Okay, good point. Yes, I will be there, too."

Livi bypassed the elevator to the underground parking, explaining as she headed to the front entrance of the building, "Someone here was having a big party tonight and the visitor parking was reserved, so I'm out at the curb."

Callan set the doughnut box on the counter in the lobby and said to the uniformed security guard, "Help yourself," as he followed Livi.

"What time is Greta supposed to be there tomorrow?" he asked as they headed for the street.

Livi told him, thinking more about that kiss they'd just shared and wondering if she was in store for another when they reached her car.

But once they got there and she'd unlocked it, he opened the door wide and held it for her to get in. Which she did, to avoid a second kiss that she told herself shouldn't happen, anyway.

Even if she was wishing it would...

"I'll have to go into my office tomorrow before the school thing," Callan said as she started her engine. "So if I'm a little late getting back here, just wait for me, okay?"

Livi nodded. Then he closed her door, tapped the roof over her head as if to signal her to go and stepped back.

Something compelled her to look at him one more time, waving as if that was the purpose of the glance.

But in truth she just wanted one last glimpse of him, to cement in her mind that while he was not Patrick, it seemed possible that Callan could be starting to take up a small place in her thoughts.

A small place that was all his own...

Chapter Seven

"Pregnant?"

"Livi..."

"How did that happen?"

"The usual way," Livi answered Lindie's last question, suffering the embarrassment of having to admit it.

Lindie and Jani had dropped in on Saturday morning. It was unusual for any of them not to see or hear from each other for a week at a time. But because Livi had taken the week off to travel to Northbridge, and since then had been so enmeshed in her own problems, on top of what she was doing with Greta Teller, she hadn't done more than text everyone that she was back. So Lindie and Jani had taken it upon themselves to check in with her.

Right in the middle of her daily bout of morning sickness.

And because they were alarmed to find her so nauseous again—or still—they'd wanted to take her to the nearest urgent care. Of course, Livi couldn't let that happen. And she'd felt too bad to keep up the facade any longer. Besides, she was well aware that she was going to have to tell her family eventually—sooner rather than later. It might as well be now.

So she'd told her sister and her cousin. Since they were also her best friends, it was where she would have started, anyway.

Their first response, after outright shock, was to hug her, tell her how happy they were with the prospect of a baby, then make her comfortable on her large, over-stuffed white sofa with pillows and a blanket. They also made her weak, decaffeinated tea and brought her soda crackers.

Once all that was done, Jani and Lindie sat in front of her on the large oak coffee table and settled in to talk.

"Have you been seeing someone and keeping it quiet?" her sister asked.

"No."

"Then who? How? When?" Lindie demanded gently.

"It's complicated…" Livi said, before she explained the whole thing, including that the man in Hawaii had turned out to be Callan Tierney—Greta's guardian.

"Fantastic!" her sister exclaimed, when she was finished.

"It is?" a confused Livi muttered.

"It is," Jani confirmed, apparently on the same wavelength with Lindie. "It's such a relief!"

"Did you guys hear me right? I don't have Patrick, I'm pregnant, the father is someone I had a one-night stand with in Hawaii and—"

"It's been four years since we lost Patrick," Lindie

said, cutting her off. "We all loved Patrick, Livi. We all miss him and will never forget him. But we've been so afraid that you were just going to let your life be over, too."

"We couldn't stand it," Jani added bluntly. "Worrying that you would go on all by yourself forever, without anyone but us. This is fate telling you no, and thank God for that!"

"Or thank GiGi," Lindie proposed. "Sometimes I think she's psychic or has magic powers or something. We all keep ending up with someone we come into contact with through these little projects of hers."

"I'm not *ending up* with Callan Tierney," Livi insisted. "I'm not even sure I'm going to tell him that the baby is his."

"Why would you not tell him?" her sister asked.

"We aren't involved with each other...like that," she said, pushing the memory of the kiss in the courtyard the night before out of her mind.

Which was not an easy thing to do when she'd been awake half the night thinking about it.

Okay, and reliving it, too.

And craving more of it. More of a lot of things she had no business craving. Or even thinking about.

"We've put Hawaii behind us," she insisted, dodging her own train of thought. "I'm writing it off to tropical fever or something. Something that caused an insane, irrational act that we've agreed to forget."

"How are you going to forget how you got this baby?" Jani reasoned. "Especially when the daddy is the guardian of this little girl you've taken under your wing? Your paths will keep crossing—what do you think he'll say when he sees you getting bigger and bigger?"

"I can always say that I had artificial insemination. Right after Hawaii. I know enough about that from when you were considering it, Jani, before you met Gideon."

"This Callan guy is king of the software business. You think he isn't bright enough to put two and two together and come up with four?" her sister said facetiously.

Livi rolled her eyes. "Of course he's *bright*, but I don't think he'll *want* to put two and two together and come up with four. I think he might be relieved with a lie that gets him off the hook on this."

Or would he? He *had* told her last night that he'd liked the idea of having a family when his wife had turned up pregnant.

But that was before he'd lost his friends, before he'd had to take over raising Greta and caring for the Tellers. Now he *did* have a family—maybe not in the traditional way, but he did—and he wasn't doing all that well with any of them. He also wasn't particularly thrilled with the situation and the demands it made on him. He was clearly uncomfortable in the role of dad, of family man. And none of it spoke in favor of adding more to his roster.

"You think he'd rather *not* know he's going to be a father?" Lindie reiterated. "If so, then he's a jerk—because I think any man who wouldn't want to know he'd fathered a baby, who would be happy to be *let off the hook* rather than have a relationship with his own child, is a jerk. At the very least."

Livi shook her head. "He's not," she said firmly. "But he *is* obsessed with his work. And he grew up hard and doesn't really relate well to a lot of people because of it. He has no concept of what it is to have a family. And he's uncomfortable with it and already juggling more than he may be able to handle. He's trying, and I think he genuinely wants to meet the obligations, but I'm not sure he can. And I'm really not sure I should pile on more. Or that I want to."

"You aren't going to try to think of this baby as Patrick's, are you?" Jani said fearfully.

Actually, it was slightly unnerving how much Patrick seemed to be fading from her thoughts, Livi realized. Not that she was forgetting him. It was just that he was somehow receding into a compartment that was separate from the present. She hadn't realized how much she'd been living in the past until the pregnancy had forced her to focus on the here and now.

But regardless of what was causing her to begin to slide Patrick off center stage, she knew it was probably for the best.

So she could honestly answer her cousin's question by saying, "No, I'm not. That would be crazy. I'm trying to think of it as *mine* and maybe mine alone."

"Don't you like this guy?" Lindie asked. "Is he just really, really gorgeous, with an irresistible body, so you let go for once, but it was only physical?"

Even her sister's general description brought the image of Callan to mind in all his glory. Yes, he was definitely gorgeous. But it wasn't only the way he looked. There was more to it. Like there had been in Hawaii, when she'd felt comfortable with him. He'd been funny, charming. Easy to talk to. And there had been a palpable chemistry between them that she'd never felt with another man. Not even Patrick.

But Livi couldn't find the words to explain any of

that, so she said, "I had a *lot* to drink, don't forget. But he is attractive."

"You're just not attracted to him when you're sober?"

"It isn't that, either."

"So you *are* attracted to him, drunk or sober," Lindie concluded.

She and Jani exchanged a knowing smile. Apparently both were satisfied with that information because they went back to their earlier position.

"Don't you think that it's the responsible thing to do—tell him he's going to be a father?" Lindie said.

"Isn't my biggest responsibility now to the baby?" Livi countered. "This guy is already on overload. He's a self-proclaimed neglector of relationships. Is it really what's best for him or me or the baby to push him into another relationship he's not equipped to handle? Wouldn't I just be setting up the baby for hurt when Callan neglects him or her, too?"

She was thinking out loud, not making any kind of decision yet, but she could tell that she'd made some valid points, because neither her sister nor her cousin said anything for a moment.

Then Lindie said, "I vote that you tell him."

"Me, too," Jani added.

But Livi thought that they were both picturing some kind of fairy tale—her telling Callan, Callan immediately dropping to one knee to propose and everyone living happily-ever-after. And Livi couldn't picture that herself. She didn't even want to.

"Callan isn't Patrick," she warned them. "Patrick was all about our marriage and the family we wanted to build. Whenever I needed him, he was there for me, one hundred percent. He wouldn't have ever done what Callan did with his ex-wife—pushing off anything to do with her onto some paid assistant. Callan had the guy stand in as a proxy for him so often, his wife ended up leaving him for the assistant."

"He delegated being a husband?" Jani asked.

"He did. And now he's delegating taking care of the older couple to the wife's nurse, and I was just on my own with Greta for the last two days because he was nowhere around."

"Yeah, that's not good..." Lindie admitted.

"But he's new to all this," Jani reminded them, though clearly some of her enthusiasm had waned.

"Sure," Livi agreed. "But he didn't figure out how to be present as a husband, even though he was married for eight years. And even if he gets the hang of looking after Greta and the Tellers, how good will he be at it? And how far can I expect him to be stretched?"

Neither woman had any answers to those questions and their expressions conceded the possibility that she might be right.

"Well, whatever way you handle this, we're behind you," Lindie said.

"All the way," Jani confirmed. Then, with a beaming smile, she said, "And we'll have another *baby*!"

"And if you end up doing it on your own, we'll be there for you every step of the way—you know that."

Livi *had* known that. But it was still a huge relief to hear for herself that they weren't judging what she'd done, that they would rally round her and that the consequences—her baby—would be as welcome as if it *was* hers and Patrick's.

But relieved or not on that count, she found it didn't change the situation she was in.

And she had no idea what to do about Callan.

The visit from her sister and cousin slowed Livi down and she ended up texting Callan to tell him that she would meet him and Greta at the private school later that day. When they arrived, kids and parents were bustling around, decorating and setting up for what they learned was to be a school sleepover that night.

During the principal's tour and basic orientation for Greta, he introduced her to several little girls who would be her classmates.

Livi was glad to see that the other nine-year-olds greeted Greta warmly. They loved her long blond hair, telling her that she looked just like an animated character they all adored.

Greta was not at all shy and responded without reservation, making what appeared to be fast friends with two of the girls. She even begged to be allowed to attend the sleepover that night when they asked her to.

Callan, appearing awkward and uncomfortable, seemed perplexed by the request and looked to Livi.

She laughed and said, "I think if she wants to go, you can probably let her. They said the school would be locked up tight, and parents will be here to supervise, so it seems safe. And someone can always call you to come and pick her up in the middle of the night if it doesn't work out."

"Can I? Can I? *Please*…" Greta begged, with beseeching doe eyes thrown in for good measure.

"Well, yeah, I guess…" Callan said uncertainly.

One of the other little girls ran to a woman helping

set up and then ran back with a sheet of paper. "This is what she'll need," the other girl announced helpfully.

Callan took the paper, staring at it and frowning.

Livi peered at the list from beside him and asked Greta if she had a sleeping bag. When she said no, Livi suggested they finish the tour, do some shopping and then stop at home for her to pack, making it back for the six o'clock lockdown.

"Yes! Yes! Yes!" Greta exclaimed, and Callan, still seeming out of his element, agreed.

"Is there really a chance that she'll call me to pick her up in the middle of the night?" Callan asked Livi after they'd walked Greta into the school again—this time for her to spend the night there.

Livi laughed. "Anything is possible. With the ten of us there were plenty of middle-of-the-night trips to pick up one or the other of us from sleepovers because we got sick or scared or couldn't sleep or whatever. That's part of being a parent."

"But for now I have the night off..." he said, as if he'd just realized that on the way to Livi's car.

Because she'd met Callan and Greta at the school, Livi had driven, too. They'd left her sedan in the school parking lot to shop and get Greta's things, but now Livi headed for it.

"You do still have the Tellers at your place," she reminded him.

"Yeah, but they already thought that Greta and I wouldn't be there for dinner. I was going to see if I could take the two of you to eat and then find an arcade, or maybe go to that fright-night thing that's running all month at the amusement park."

"Really? You planned a kid thing?"

"I did," he said, as if he was proud of himself for it. "And since I told the Tellers not to expect us tonight, they decided to have a marathon of some crime show they like. So how about I treat you to dinner—to say thanks for all you did for Greta this last week, and for coming today?"

"But no arcade or fright-night?" she joked, as if she was disappointed.

"Well, we *could* do either one of those. But it seems like a nice dinner says thank-you better..."

A thank-you dinner, not a date.

Once Livi convinced herself that that distinction existed, she considered the invitation. It didn't take long.

"I don't have any other plans," she said. "But nothing fancy." Because fancy would seem like a date.

"Sushi?"

The obstetrician had said no raw fish.

"I like sushi, but I'm not in the mood..."

"There's a good Mexican food place in LoDo?"

Not living far from there, Livi was familiar with the lower downtown historic district referred to as LoDo. "I'm a fan of Mexican food."

"Then Tamayo it is. Why don't I follow you to your place to leave your car?"

Callan was in tan slacks and a red-and-cream-colored sport shirt that were nice enough for the restaurant. Indian summer temperatures had allowed for black pants and a lightweight white sweater set for Livi—and she knew that was dressy enough for that particular restaurant, too. Which meant she didn't need to change, either, and could have offered to just meet him there.

But the thought of not fighting traffic or parking was appealing, and she ended up agreeing to his suggestion.

It was nearly seven by the time they got to the restaurant. It was packed, but the hostess recognized Callan and they were seated at a secluded corner table right away.

Livi refused wine or any other liquor—again on obstetrician's orders—and insisted sparkling water was all she wanted, so Callan didn't drink, either. Then they studied the menu, made their choices and were left to share guacamole and tortilla chips.

"You must come here a lot for the hostess to know you," Livi said then.

"I do. But I also went out with her—twice, I think."

Livi couldn't help taking a second look at the other woman. She was taller than Livi, model-skinny, with coal-black hair, pale skin and dramatic makeup. Pretty but severe.

And as with Kinsey, Livi didn't like the idea of Callan with someone else, even though she knew it shouldn't matter to her.

"She doesn't seem to have any hard feelings," she observed.

"She turned me down for what would have been the third date. Or maybe the fourth, I'm not really sure. It was right after my divorce, but there were weeks in between our dates—"

"Because you were working," Livi guessed.

"Yep. And even those dates never happened when they were supposed to. They were rescheduled a couple times each because I got busy. So the last time I had my secretary call her—"

"Your secretary makes your dates for you?"

"She didn't make the first one—that happened one night when I came in here late and Dray just sort of joined me."

"So, like your ex-wife who scheduled herself into your free time, this one did the pursuing, too?"

"There wasn't much pursuit. I think she was just bored and I was alone and sitting at the table nearest to the hostess station, so she struck up a conversation and it went from there. But it didn't go very far. When my secretary called her again, she said no. There had been too much time between dates and she'd met someone else."

And he didn't seem to care about that. Which made Livi feel better on the one hand. But on the other hand, it was another relationship—however brief—that he'd let fizzle through neglect, and she couldn't help noting that.

"Greta surprised me today," Callan said then. "I thought she'd be afraid or worried about starting a new school, so she'd hang back. But she jumped right in, didn't she?"

"She did. But she's outgoing and that's good for her. Believe me. I was just the opposite and it was miserable."

"You were shy and withdrawn?" he asked, sounding surprised.

Which of course he would be, she realized. Not only because of Hawaii, but because she did feel comfortable enough with him for her shy side not to show.

"I was *horribly* shy and withdrawn as a kid," she said, omitting how often that was still the case. "When I was Greta's age, if I'd had to change schools, I would have been a mess. I wouldn't have even been able to think of something to say to those two girls Greta made instant friends with, and I would *not* have had the courage to go to that sleepover tonight. I was a mouse."

"No kidding?"

"No kidding. In fact, that's what some mean kids used

to call me—Mouse—because I was so timid. I was actually miserable in school until the sixth grade."

"What happened in the sixth grade?" Callan asked.

He seemed genuinely interested. The way he always did when they were together. His attentiveness didn't seem in keeping with someone who often disregarded relationships.

But in spite of seeing that, appreciating it, she had a bigger issue on her mind—telling him about Patrick.

There wasn't a reason not to, though. So she said, "In sixth grade, I met my husband."

Callan laughed. "Was it some kind of arranged thing? A joining of two powerful families through the marriage of their kids?"

Their tortilla soups arrived and after the waiter had left again, Livi said, "No, Patrick just moved here from North Carolina with his family and joined the class."

"And changed your world?" Callan said, still with some doubt in his voice.

"Kind of. I'd been in school with the same kids since preschool—a private school that was also near GiGi, so that didn't change when we went to live with her. My siblings and my cousins were my only friends, and everyone else in school either overlooked me altogether because I was so quiet, or teased me unmercifully. Then Patrick came in—"

"That's your husband's name—Patrick?"

"It was."

Callan paused in eating his soup and looked at her. "It *was* his name? He changed it? I mean, I've been assuming you're divorced…"

Livi shook her head. "I said I wasn't married anymore, I didn't say I was divorced. Patrick passed away."

And while her voice cracked just slightly when she said that, for the first time she managed to get the words out without tearing up.

Callan's surprise showed in his expression. "I didn't think that... At our age you just automatically go to divorce. Car accident?"

Livi shook her head again. "Four years ago—a month after our fifth anniversary—Patrick was playing basketball with my brothers and cousins. And then he just dropped—died on the spot of an undiagnosed brain aneurysm."

Callan's eyebrows shot up. "Seriously?"

"Seriously."

She hadn't had to tell this story in a long while and was pleasantly surprised to discover herself able to do it less emotionally than she ever had before.

Whether because Callan was easy to talk to or because of that comfort level she'd realized she had with him, it was a relief not to have to relive the agony the way she had in the past.

Not that she didn't still feel the sadness, the underlying grief, but to be able to talk about it without breaking down was a big step for her.

"Geez, Livi, I'm sorry. That must have been a shock," Callan said gently.

"Oh, yeah," she answered with a small, mirthless laugh. "To say the least. We'd been together almost since the first day he walked into my sixth-grade classroom. There was never any sign that he wasn't healthy as a horse and—" she took a deep breath "—I never doubted that we'd be together forever, that we'd grow old together."

There was a moment of silence—some of it taken up by their waiter replenishing their water. Then Cal-

Ian backed the conversation up. "So Patrick came into your sixth-grade class and everything changed for you?"

"Patrick was..." She shook her head and chuckled briefly. "Even as a kid he was personable. He was a cutup who made everyone laugh. Everybody loved him. He fit in everywhere he went. I never met anyone who *didn't* like him—"

"And he liked the quiet little girl in the corner."

That was a nice way to put it. "He did. Don't ask me why he even noticed me, but he did."

"And tell me he beat up the mean kids who called you Mouse, so they left you alone."

That made her laugh again. "He defended me, but he was a little guy—shorter than I was in sixth grade and not tall or bulky even after puberty—so he didn't get into fights. He actually would just head off the mean teasing by joking around with the bullies. What he did for me was more along the lines of drawing me *out* of the corner by bolstering my confidence and getting me to participate. Eventually I lived down the nickname."

"He showed everyone that you were smart and funny and amazing yourself, even if you were hiding it?"

Was that what Callan thought of her?

It felt good to think he might.

"Patrick just helped bring me out of my shell and that changed things."

"So you married him—when? Seventh? Eighth grade?" Callan joked as his chipotle-rubbed pork chops and her carnitas were served.

"I might as well have."

"Come on... Really?" he said, as if he thought she had to be exaggerating.

"Really. Puppy love through sixth and into seventh

grade. After that, when our friends were starting to have boyfriends or girlfriends, we officially became that—a couple. And we were a couple to the end."

Callan's eyebrows rose again.

"I know, it sounds kind of weird," Livi said, seeing his astonishment. "But once we were together that was just *it* for us. It sounds corny, but we really were two halves that made a whole, and even though we discovered each other as kids, we both believed it was just meant to be."

"The soul-mate thing?" He sounded skeptical.

But Livi said definitively, "Yes. I felt it. Patrick felt it. He was my one-and-only, and I was his."

"And that's all she wrote? You were *together* from the sixth grade on? There wasn't even any on-again, off-again?"

"None. Through grade school and college."

"You went to the same one?"

"Oh, yeah, so we could stay together. There was never a question about that. We got married the week after we graduated, and Patrick went to law school at Denver University while I took my place at Camden Incorporated."

"He was a lawyer?"

"He passed the bar the first time," she said with pride.

Callan was looking at her as if seeing something he hadn't witnessed before. "So it was a real love story," he marveled.

"Kind of like your friendship with Greta's mom and dad. Or their relationship with each other."

He laughed. "I never thought of a friendship as a love story, but I guess I can see the similarities. But when it comes to Mandy and J.J., they didn't get together until after they'd both done the kind of dating around that everyone did. It wasn't love from the sixth grade on. And that two-halves-of-a-whole thing? That one-and-only stuff? I'm not sure even Mandy or J.J. thought of each other that way. I mean, they were great together, but…" He shook his head. "I don't know about *that*."

The waiter came to take their plates and Callan enticed Livi into sharing a dessert.

Once they were alone again, he said, "Since Mandy and J.J. died I've felt kind of like I've lost my safety net or something. But you…you must have felt like you lost a limb."

"I think I kind of felt like I lost all four," she said. "I don't remember much of the first year—I was just a zombie so it's a blur. And it's been a slow climb since then."

"But you're okay now?"

"I think I am. It's been a long road and grief still dances me around the room every once in a while, but that's pretty rare. All in all, I'm back to myself."

"And dating and…" He frowned as something seemed to occur to him. "Hawaii wasn't your first…*date*…since your husband?" he said, as if it couldn't possibly be true.

Their dessert came before she had to answer him.

It was a flourless brownie topped with chocolate ice cream and a layer of salted caramel, glazed with white chocolate before a blood-orange reduction was drizzled over it all. And remembering that he hadn't opted for a chocolate doughnut the night before, she appreciated that he'd recalled her love for chocolate and ordered with that in mind.

Livi took a spoonful from her side of the confection and oohed and aahed over it while he continued watching her.

She was afraid he was waiting to have his question

answered, and encouraged him to dig in, hoping to distract him.

It failed.

"Come on," he said. "Was Hawaii a first for you?"

"I thought we were forgetting about Hawaii?" she hedged, uncomfortable talking about it.

"So that's a yes—it was," he answered, as if he'd read it on her face.

"Patrick was a very tough act to follow," she said quietly.

And yet Callan had...

For some reason, that was the first time she'd attributed what had happened in Hawaii to him and not to the liquor or the setting or the anniversary insanity.

But she didn't want to think too much about that, so she didn't.

She merely said, "You don't go from what Patrick and I had, from what he was to me, and just dive in to...well, to just anything. I didn't know if I'd ever be able to... *date*. Then Hawaii—" she shrugged "—just happened."

So naturally...

Livi took refuge in her second bite of chocolate.

"I don't know whether to be honored or...not," Callan said, frowning again.

He finally tried their dessert. Livi had the impression that he was using it to buy himself a little time to think. To consider if he did or didn't like the position he'd now found himself in.

Then, as if he'd decided to put a positive spin on it, he said, "So I brought out a little something in you, too?"

Him and her anniversary and a lot of booze.

But now that she was adding him to the list, she couldn't

deny that—like Patrick—Callan *had* brought something out in her.

"I guess so," she admitted, more under her breath than not, because realizing it was slightly unnerving. Callan and Patrick were *not* alike. So why did she respond to Callan in some of the same ways? Especially when there was so much about him that didn't recommend him?

"So can I assume—considering Hawaii—that you at least aren't some long-suffering widow who's thrown herself on her late husband's pyre?" he asked then.

"I'm not exactly sure what I am these days."

Pregnant—that's what she was.

"Because who could compete with a guy like you lost," Callan guessed. "Let alone some stranger you just met on a beach. But you ended up in my hotel room anyway, and that doesn't fit."

He was perceptive. And right.

But at that moment she didn't like the sense that he could see into her head.

"I didn't think anyone could compete with Patrick, no," she said.

"Past tense? You've changed your mind?"

Sometimes it seemed it was changing on its own.

But she didn't want to admit that, so she only said, "I'm still in flux in some ways. I thought..." Livi shrugged again. "I just thought I'd settled in to the way things would be from here on."

"Being a widow? Alone? You didn't think you'd ever find anyone else or *be with* anyone else?"

"It just didn't seem...likely," she admitted.

"Ever?"

"I couldn't picture it ever happening, no. But Hawaii... confused things."

"Because you found out that you're still alive and well and kicking."

She shrugged once again, thinking—reluctantly—that in four years that *had* happened only with him. And that just made it more confusing.

Too confusing for her to want to keep exploring right then.

They'd finished their dessert and Callan had paid the check, so Livi pointed out that with a crowd of people still waiting for a table, they should probably go.

Their conversation seemed to have left Callan with a lot on his mind, too, because he was less talkative than usual as he drove his SUV back to her house. They chatted a little about Greta and if she would make it through the night at the sleepover, but not much else.

Then they reached Livi's two-story, white, Cape Cod style house.

Callan walked her to her door and along the way she fretted.

She was inclined to ask him in. But she was also worried about what it would be like if he accepted. How would she feel if she brought a man into the house she and Patrick had designed and built and lived in together?

But before she'd resolved her dilemma, Callan said, "I suppose I'd better get home. Even though Greta is gone for the night, I still have the Tellers there. And since I was in trouble last night for not going home..."

Livi seized that excuse and agreed that it was probably best for him to limit his time away.

Then she said, "My family has a big Sunday dinner every week at my grandmother's house. GiGi asked me to invite you and Greta and the Tellers tomorrow. It's a whole lot of Camdens, but there's always other people, too. And good food. GiGi thought it might be a way for the Tellers to get out a little, to meet some folks their own age. Kinsey is included in the invitation, so she could still look after Maeve, and there's plenty of room for the wheelchair. I just didn't know if there was any chance you might risk consorting with even more of us..."

And why did she sound—and feel—so hopeful that there was a chance?

"I think I can take the risk," Callan said facetiously. "But I'll have to run it by the troops. Can I text you when I know where everyone stands?"

Not an immediate acceptance, but not a no, either.

"Sure."

She should have said good-night then, but there she was, lingering, gazing up at him in the glow of her porch light, wondering why he had to be so great-looking with all those chiseled angles of his face and those dark eyes and that hair...

He was studying her just as intently when a small smile appeared. "So..." he said, his voice lower and more confidential. "I'll try not to let it go to my head."

"You'll try not to let *what* go to your head?"

"You know—I might not be *the* one-and-only, but I am the one-and-only guy in the last four years to wake up Sleeping Beauty. I mean, look at you—there have to be a lot of single guys lined up hoping for a shot with you."

"Not that I'm aware of."

"Because you were Sleeping Beauty and were focused on dealing with your own stuff. But trust me, they've been there waiting for a chance and you just haven't noticed."

It was nice that he thought so, but she didn't agree. Instead of arguing, though, she goaded, "You've decided you're one in a million, but you're trying not to let it go to your head."

His smile turned into a grin that wasn't even slightly humble. "Hey, don't take away the little bit of one-and-only status I have. I'm playing out of my league, up against the memory of the greatest guy who ever lived."

He said that as if it was a fact, without any sarcasm, and since it was the way Livi knew she'd portrayed Patrick, she didn't take offense.

She also didn't tell Callan that in some ways Patrick wasn't in *his* league...

She'd worn her hair loose, the way she usually did, and he raised a hand to the side of her face, smoothing back a strand. Then his hands ended up on her shoulders, squeezing firmly, comfortingly, consolingly. But there was more than that to the touch, too—a sensuality. Or maybe she was imagining things.

But she wasn't imagining how good it felt to have those big, capable hands on her.

"I'm sorry for the tragedies and losses that hurt you," Callan said in a quiet voice. "But I can't say I'm sorry that it landed us here..."

Here, where his big hands steadied her as he leaned forward and kissed her.

He pulled her to him once his mouth was on hers, wrapping her in his arms as his lips parted and the kiss deepened.

It was such a powerhouse of a kiss that it actually washed away all that they'd talked about tonight. And everything else that had brought them there, leaving Livi with her eyes closed and her mind adrift, lost to everything but the feel of his lips urging hers to part, too.

She was aware only of his arms around her, holding

her tight, bolstering her when that kiss weakened her knees. Of the intoxicating scent of his cologne. Of how very good he was at kissing—so good that she didn't think twice about welcoming his tongue when it came to greet hers. About accepting and reciprocating that added intimacy.

Her hands went from his chest around to his back, and that allowed him to bring her in closer still, holding her against him, showing her suddenly how sensitive her breasts were. And how nice it felt to have them burrowing into him.

For a while she even forgot that they were standing on her front porch, out in the open, under the spotlight of the lanterns on either side of her door where any of her neighbors could see. There was only his mouth on hers, his muscular arms holding her, their bodies pressed together as their tongues toyed with each other.

Until the sound of a car driving down her street made her remember with just enough of a jolt for Callan to register it.

Still, his tongue didn't bid hers a hasty farewell. Instead it was a reluctant one, retreating and letting that kiss become softer and sweeter before he brought it to a conclusion. Then returned to kiss her again. And again.

And even after that he didn't let go of her. He kept holding her while he looked down into her eyes and she looked up into his.

After another moment he took a long pull of air that raised his shoulders, and then dropped them with his exhale. Clearly, he wasn't happy accepting the fact that the night had to end. "Isn't there supposed to be some kind of appeal to having people to go home to?" he joked.

"There is," Livi confirmed, even though the last thing she wanted at that moment was for him to leave.

"So...I should do it."

"You should."

He kissed her again, a long, deep kiss that caused her to think about stepping into the shadows of her porch, where they wouldn't be so much on display and could keep kissing awhile longer.

But then he ended that kiss, too, and took his arms from around her. "I'll text you about tomorrow," he promised.

Livi nodded and opened her door. But even with one hand on the knob she didn't go in. She stood there and watched Callan return to his car, drinking in the sight of him, before she closed the door between them.

Then she stood in her entryway, looking around at the house she alone occupied, and imagining what it would have been like if Callan *had* come in.

But while she expected that image to have a negative impact on her, for it not to feel right, she discovered something entirely different.

She found she *could* picture Callan there.

And more than that, she was wishing he was...

Chapter Eight

"Oh. Hey. Morning," Callan said when he came out of his at-home office on Sunday for his second cup of coffee. He was surprised to find John Sr. sitting on one of the bar stools at the island counter in the kitchen.

"You up before me again?" the older man grumbled, as if it was a competition he resented losing.

"Work to do," Callan answered tersely, leaving out the part where he was having trouble sleeping because Livi was occupying his mind.

After that kiss on her porch last night he'd been even more stirred up and wide-awake and restless than every other night since they'd reconnected in Northbridge. Finally, he'd just given up the fight and decided to get something accomplished rather than go on trying to sleep, wrestling with thoughts he knew he shouldn't be having.

"Guess you didn't get all you got layin' 'round in bed," the older man concluded.

There *was* a scenario in which Callan would have liked to be lying around in bed. But it included Livi. Without Livi and alone there, thinking about her, wanting to repeat Hawaii so bad it was nearly driving him crazy, he found his bed was like a torture chamber these days.

But while that was something he would have said to J.J., it certainly wasn't something he would say to John Sr. So instead he asked, "How come you're up so early without cows to milk and animals to feed?"

"Habit. Don't even need an alarm clock anymore."

Callan nodded toward the mug on the counter in front of John Sr. "Got your coffee okay?"

"Yep."

"I just came out for my second."

The elderly man made no comment and Callan went around the island to the coffeemaker while silence hung in the air.

Instantly, Livi was on his mind again.

But this time he wasn't thinking about how shiny her hair was or how blue her eyes were. About how much he liked the sound of her voice, her laugh, how soft her skin was or how much he wanted to get his hands on her. He wasn't thinking that he had no business thinking any of that, given that he was fresh out of a marriage he'd tanked, and had his hands full with the Tellers and Greta. He wasn't even thinking that Livi was a Camden and he should be trying for distance from her rather than the opposite.

This time he was thinking about the things she'd said to him on Friday night. And he knew that if she saw what was going on between him and John Sr. at that moment, she'd blame Callan for dropping the ball, missing a chance to break some ice.

And he knew she would be right.

So once his coffee was ready, rather than taking it back to his office, he turned to drink it standing at the island facing John Sr.

Who scowled and stared at him through narrowed eyes as if he was up to something.

Callan ignored the suspicious glare. But seeing it and knowing the man, he also paused a moment to consider what he was going to say before he said it. Because he knew that if he didn't handle this conversation delicately he could aggravate him, injure that pride Livi had talked about and do more harm than good.

So Callan considered carefully before he said, "I'm thinking that I could use help with some things."

"That so?"

"It is. Greta needs to be taken to school in the mornings and picked up in the afternoons. And I'm guessing there will be supplies she'll have to have for projects that come up, and times she wants to go to friends' houses or after-school things and will need rides. She'll probably have to be taken to a doctor or the dentist now and then— all of it during my work hours. And there's Maeve—I know how she likes to cook and I'm looking forward to coming home to that when she gets well. But I also know she'll need trips to the grocery store and what not."

"There can be a lot of running around, that's for sure," John Sr. agreed.

"So I was wondering if you would, uh, consider taking care of stuff like that if we got you a car and I showed you around, got you familiar with streets and routes to everywhere?"

Even though it didn't seem possible, John Sr.'s eyes narrowed even more and bored through him assessingly.

Callan expected the worst. A tirade about how the elderly man didn't need anyone buying him a car and wasn't taking any charity. About how he didn't need to be shown how to drive anywhere as if he was a punk kid with a new driver's license. About how Callan was asking him to do his own job as guardian, because Callan was a lazy, no-good something or other.

But instead, after a moment, John Sr.'s bushy gray eyebrows arched a little and he said, "I could probably do that."

Feeling as if a door had opened a crack, Callan nudged it a bit wider. "I'm sure there's a branch around here of that lodge you used to go to in Northbridge—wheels would get you there, too. You might find yourself a poker game."

"Need to keep up my membership in the Cattlemen's Association, too," he said.

"Sure. I guess there are meetings and whatever. Maybe they could use a man like you during the Stock Show…"

"Happy to lend a hand," the elderly man said, in a way that didn't make it clear whether he was happy to lend a hand to Callan or the Cattlemen's Association.

Callan thought it was more likely the latter, but what *he* was happy about was that John Sr. was so willingly—in his own way—accepting Livi's idea of getting him driving again here.

"Think about what kind of car you'd like to have," Callan said then. "Something heavy and able to get you around even in the winter snow. I have a car guy we can go see…maybe tomorrow night?"

"Got nothin' else planned."

But the elderly man did seem to have a new attitude. He almost looked chipper. At least as chipper as Callan had ever seen him.

"Great," Callan said with some relief. "I figure we're all family now and whatever it takes to get things done, we'll get them done—together."

"Makes sense."

"Good then…" Callan was stumped for anything else to say. He'd already talked to the Tellers about Sunday dinner at the Camdens when he'd come home last night, and they wanted to go. Livi hadn't given him a game plan for more than talking to John Sr. about a car, so he was at a loss. And certainly John Sr. didn't seem to have any more to say.

So Callan decided to take his win and go. "I should probably get back to work."

The elderly man didn't speak. He merely raised his chin in acknowledgment.

Without another word between them, Callan took his coffee and headed to his office.

But he still counted what had just happened as a step forward. Maybe only a small one, but still a step.

And it was thanks to Livi.

Who was on his mind again by the time he closed his office door behind him.

"I don't know, Mandy," he said to the memory of his friend. "She might be a Camden, but she's great with Greta and your in-laws—not to mention she's doing me some good. So far I can't find much to fault her."

He knew what his friend would say if she were there to answer him—that the Camdens started out looking good and then pulled the rug out from under the people who trusted them when it suited them.

But the more he got to know Livi, the more he thought he might have to argue that with Mandy—even though she'd have argued back that his opinion was colored by the fact that he had the hots for Livi something fierce.

And that would be where he'd lose the argument.

Because he couldn't deny it.

But still, he knew he needed to find a way to curb what was going on in him when it came to the lovely Livi Camden.

He had enough to deal with trying to figure out how to be a surrogate dad to Greta and a surrogate son to Maeve, and even to John Sr.

And they had to come first.

Livi thought that Sunday dinner at her grandmother's house with Callan, Greta, the Tellers and Kinsey went well.

Greta had had a great time at her school sleepover and was full of stories of her new friends to share with Livi, before she went off to play with Livi's nephew Carter.

Kinsey mainly stayed by Maeve's side to look after her, but even in the course of that, the nurse still chatted a little with everyone and seemed to enjoy herself.

Maeve, John Sr., GiGi and GiGi's new husband, Jonah—who was also originally from Northbridge—reminisced about growing up in the small town. GiGi persuaded Maeve to join the book club she and Margaret belonged to, and even gave her a copy of the book being read currently so Maeve could catch up.

And John Sr. connected with Louie over talk of Louie's garden and yard, and what Louie preferred in a vehicle for getting around the city during the winter months.

For Livi, the evening was a mixed bag.

Jani and Lindie had promised they wouldn't tell the rest of their family about Livi's pregnancy. But Livi had no doubt that Jani had told her husband, Gideon, and that Lindie had told Sawyer, her fiancé. And with Callan also at the dinner, Livi worried that someone would make a slip, that the news might get out and Callan might hear it.

Running interference just in case, she stayed close to him throughout the evening as he met everyone and hit it off with her brothers and male cousins over the Broncos and football.

She told herself that maintaining her position by Callan's side while she suffered through the football talk really was purely a safety measure. But in all honesty… she didn't want to be anywhere else.

Especially when she discovered that being at Sunday dinner with someone for the first time in four years wasn't awkward or uncomfortable, the way she'd thought it would be.

Instead, she actually enjoyed being there with Callan and sort of being part of a twosome again—although she certainly didn't consider them a *couple*. And as much as she liked Sunday dinner ordinarily, having him there with her to share it all somehow made it even better.

But it was still a weight off her shoulders to walk out GiGi's front door, certain that her secret had been kept. And as nice as the evening was, she was glad when it was over.

Livi had driven Greta and Kinsey to the dinner so Maeve could have the backseat of Callan's SUV to herself to accommodate her broken leg. And when they returned to the condo, Greta wanted Livi's help choosing an outfit to wear for her first day of school, so she didn't merely drop off the nine-year-old and the nurse when she got them home. She went up to Callan's condo with everyone else.

Once she and Greta were in Greta's bedroom, not only did the little girl want advice on her clothes and shoes, she wanted to discuss hairstyles, too. And her backpack. And what to do at lunch. And she lamented that she didn't have pierced ears when *everyone* else did, and wanted Livi to draw earrings on her with a marker—an idea Livi nixed. To compensate, she lent the girl two of the beaded bracelets she was wearing.

Although it was clear that the sleepover had gone well and Greta was excited about starting school, Livi could see that she was also nervous. So even after all the fashion decisions had been made she stayed with Greta, urging her to put on her pajamas and brush her teeth. Then she read to her to get her mind off the day to come, not leaving her until Greta was dozing off.

Then Livi quietly slipped out of the room, closing the door behind her.

The condo was so quiet that she wondered if everyone had forgotten she was there and had gone to bed.

But when she got to the open-concept living space and kitchen, Callan was there. Waiting, it seemed, because he was standing at the bank of windows in the living room area, looking out over Denver.

She'd been so careful about not making any noise to disturb Greta that he didn't hear her coming. So for a moment Livi stopped and did what she'd wanted to do all night and hadn't out of fear that someone might notice—she just took in the sight of him. There, in the quiet of his condominium, with no one else around and him unaware she was doing it, she feasted a little, getting the front view of his reflection in the glass, along with the rear view, too. From the back she got to look at broad shoulders that tapered down to a narrow waist and a derriere that those pants loved.

There was no denying that the man was male-model gorgeous, with a body any designer would die to dress. And even though she tried not to, Livi couldn't help wishing once again that she hadn't been such a stickler about having the hotel room in Hawaii so dark that she hadn't had a real look at him in the buff…

He turned from the window and she went the rest of the way into the room, as if she hadn't paused to stare.

"That took a while," he observed, apparently none the wiser.

"We girls can't go out in just anything," she joked.

"The Tellers crashed—looks like we wore them out— and Kinsey left. But it isn't that late… Sit a minute?"

"Okay," she agreed, before she'd even had the time to ponder it, rationalize it, justify it. Following only the impulse to have some time alone with him.

"Wine?" he offered.

Under other circumstances, yes.

"No, thanks. I'm at my limit tonight for food and drink."

"Then just come and sit."

She did, going to the big leather sofa, where he joined her, both of them near the center, angled toward each other. Callan relaxed with an arm along the top of the cushions, an ankle resting atop the opposite knee.

"Was dinner too much for Maeve?" Livi asked as they settled in.

"I don't think so. They were both glad they went— they said so on the drive home. And they're looking forward to getting out again and doing stuff with people their own age—you were right about that. Maeve couldn't wait to dive into that book, and John Sr. offered to help Louie winterize the yard and garden. He's thrilled with the idea of getting his hands dirty."

"Once a farmer always a farmer?"

"I think so," Callan confirmed, before he changed the subject. "Louie and Margaret—they're the people who started out as staff and then helped raise you, right?"

"Right. They're my grandmother's best friends."

"And Jonah—he's her husband and he grew up in Northbridge, too?"

"He and GiGi were high school sweethearts who went their separate ways and then reconnected just recently here in Denver. They've only been married since June."

"Well, the Tellers said they felt at home with your grandmother and her husband, and with Margaret and Louie, too. So doing this tonight was a great idea. Thanks."

"I can't take the credit. It wasn't my idea…" And it wasn't something she would have suggested on her own, because she'd been worried about being there with a man who wasn't Patrick, and about someone spilling the beans about the baby. "It was GiGi who extended the invitation. I was just the messenger. But I'm glad it worked out." She paused and then said, "And what's this I overheard about John Sr. getting a car?"

Callan smiled, pleased with himself. "We talked early this morning. I used the same angle on him that you used on me."

"Angle?" Livi repeated, pretending to take offense at the word.

"You know, that stuff about how if John Sr. had wheels it would help me out?"

"That wasn't an angle," she insisted, even though it had been. "It was the truth."

"Yeah, but it was an angle, too. To make me see your point. But I *did* see your point and I thought it was a good approach to take to protect the old man's pride—also what you said needed to be done."

"Is this you giving me—a *Camden*—credit for something?" she challenged.

"It is. And also I'm giving you a hard time," he said, again pleased with himself.

"But you and John Sr. actually had a conversation?"

Callan nodded. "I think you could call it that. Enough to get the job done, anyway."

"You know it's only a start, though, right? I mean, you need to keep up a dialogue to actually *build* a relationship. One conversation doesn't do it."

"Yeah, yeah, yeah. But this *was* a beginning and I think I made a little headway—how about you give *me* some credit?"

Livi laughed. "Good job!" she praised, the way she might have praised a puppy in training.

But Callan didn't seem to care. He merely smiled, bowed his head as if humbly accepting an award and said, "Thank you."

She laughed at him.

He raised his head again and for some reason that simple movement caused her to hone in on his neck. Exposed to just below his Adam's apple, it was thick and strong, and from out of nowhere she suddenly thought that it was very sexy. And she had the oddest inclination to kiss it…

Shying away from her own wandering thoughts, she said, "What about you? Did you have a good time tonight?"

He looked very pointedly at her. "I did have a good time," he said, as if she was the reason for it.

"Did it convince you that we aren't evildoers and villains?"

He smiled again. "What would Sunday dinner with evildoers and villains be like? Surely they wouldn't want to give themselves away as evildoers and villains, would they?"

"You just think we were on our best behavior?"

"Well, it *was* Sunday dinner—how much evildoing and villainy would go on there?"

Livi rolled her eyes and shook her head. Obviously, he was feeling ornery tonight. But she didn't mind. She was enjoying it. Him. As usual...

"So if you still believe we're treacherous," she said then, "are you going to chaperone the book club and the yard winterizing to make sure Maeve and John Sr. are safe from Camden duplicity, too?"

Callan sighed dramatically. "Maybe I'll just have to hire bodyguards," he said, with a Cheshire cat smile that let her know he was kidding.

Even so, Livi reached across him to pinch his biceps.

"Hey!" he protested.

"Do you really still think we're horrible people you have to be careful of?" she demanded.

"The story of Mandy's dad is pretty compelling stuff," he reminded her.

"That you aren't going to ever let me live down?"

Callan smiled crookedly and a sparkle came into his dark eyes. "The jury is still out, but it's leaning in your favor. You might not want complete exoneration, though," he said enticingly. "I have to admit that to the old troublemaker in me, there's some appeal in flirting with danger."

"That's me, all right—pure danger," she said wryly.

"With your family background? You might not be *pure* danger, but there's an element there," he said, his voice slightly quieter, as if even a small element of it intrigued him.

Livi didn't think she'd ever before felt as if she was intriguing to anyone. Patrick and she had been close even before they'd reached puberty, so there was nothing unknown between them. And it pleased her that with Callan there was some mystery about her. It actually inspired her to be a little bolder. The way she had been in Hawaii.

"So I guess you'd better watch yourself," she warned.

His smile grew wicked. "I'd rather watch *you*," he muttered, just as he leaned forward to kiss her.

And deep down Livi recognized that this was really why she'd been so willing to come in tonight. Really why she'd stayed. Since the moment Callan had left her porch last night all she'd wanted was to kiss him again. And now she had her wish.

It was a simple kiss at first. Chaste and sweet—like on Friday night in the courtyard, except tonight he wasn't touching her at all.

But it stayed that way only for a moment before lips parted and tongues took to frolicking the way they had the previous evening. First with delirious happiness at meeting again, before their dance slowed to something more languorous, more mature and sumptuous and erotic.

Was this what Callan had been aiming for tonight, too? she wondered, somehow having the sense that it was.

He moved his left hand from the sofa cushion, sneaking under her hair to her nape. Then up to cradle her head as mouths opened more and that kiss dived to new depths.

The arm she'd pinched came around her, pulling her up against him—closer tonight. Close enough for her to register even more strongly how incredibly sensitive pregnancy had made her breasts.

Her nipples turned into knots within the confines of her lacy bra and it was as if they were demanding not to be neglected.

And suddenly Livi was nothing but a jumble of demands being made by a body that had taken over her brain, canceling every thought and leaving her a mass of sensations and needs and longings and cravings.

She couldn't get enough of Callan kissing her, of the feel of one of his hands in her hair, the other massaging her back.

Her own arms had gone around him and she couldn't get enough of the feel of his back beneath her palms, either. She wanted more, so she found the bottom of that sweater and finessed her way under it so flesh could meet flesh.

Every hill, every valley, every muscle and tendon of that oh-so-masculine and muscular back—she memorized it all with her hands. She couldn't press her fingers firmly enough into him, massaging and kneading, mimicking what she wanted him to be doing to her front.

Her front that ached with the driving need to feel his hands there as their mouths plundered each other, leaving her awash in a desire more intense than she could ever remember feeling.

Finally taking the hint, Callan dragged a palm to one of her breasts. Even through her blouse and bra, his cupping it sent a flash flood of even more longing through her, making her groan softly. After only a few caresses, he slipped his hand into the overlapping wrap blouse and down inside the cup of her bra.

Livi couldn't contain the gasp that came from her throat at that.

She hadn't found much to enjoy in pregnancy. So far, it had made her sick every morning, and tired and sluggish throughout the day. It had made her overly affected by simple smells and sometimes weepy when she least expected. But that was all before Callan's big hand formed the perfect mold for a breast that was so alive with sensation that she saw stars.

All on their own, her spine arched and her breasts expanded into his grip. And as he began to press firm fingers into her flesh, to knead and release, to tenderly pinch and twist her nipple and then let it nestle into his palm again, Livi felt the rise of even more demanding desires shouting to be satisfied.

But where?

They were at his place. They could go to his bedroom. Like they'd gone to his hotel room in Hawaii...

And then what? Would they wake Greta or the Tellers? Would she cross paths with one of his housemates afterward? Would they somehow find out she was there, making love with Callan?

The thought quenched the desire in her just enough to clear her head.

She wanted him. More, Livi thought, than she had in Hawaii. More than she could remember wanting even Patrick.

But not here. Not worrying and sneaking around

Callan's new family. Not in any way that might leave her with another round of regrets and shame.

She yanked her head free of that kiss and covered his hand at her breast with her own. But despite intending to pull that away, too, she somehow ended up pressing it tighter to her.

Still she whispered, "We can't do this here."

"Like two teenage kids hoping not to get caught?" he said, as if he'd read her mind.

He kissed her again before she could answer, and Livi continued to hold his hand to her breast, wanting so badly not to let it go, not to end the contact.

But then he ended that kiss, too, and withdrew his hand from inside her blouse.

"I get it," he said with a resigned sigh. "But I gotta tell you it makes for a *really* big negative to having other people in my house…"

Livi was focused on trying to tame her own raging desires and didn't comment on that. Instead, after taking a deep breath to gain some control, she said, "I should go."

The look on Callan's handsome face told her how much he hated that idea, but he didn't say anything to stop her. He merely stood up and held out his hand for her to take.

She almost didn't want to, because touching him in any way at all seemed like an invitation back into what had been so difficult to end already.

But somehow her hand went to his.

As he walked her out of his condo, to the elevator and then through the parking garage, he kept her close to his side.

"Next Saturday night is a dinner-slash-silent-auction my company does for charity every year," he said as they approached her car. "My ex-wife used to plan it, but my new assistant and secretary have taken it over. I still have to attend, though, and I hate to go alone. Any chance that you'd keep me company? It's for a good cause—it goes to college scholarships for underprivileged kids, and we take the total raised by the auction and match it."

This definitely sounded like a date. After what had just happened—on top of what had happened in Hawaii—Livi's better judgment told her to say no.

But her hand was so snug in his and what had just happened had left her a little floaty—and she'd already exhausted all the willpower she had access to tonight when she'd first pulled away...

Livi heard herself say, "If it's for a good cause..." as if that mattered at the moment, when what she was really thinking was how much she didn't want him to let go of her, to send her on her way.

"Great," he said. "Now I can look forward to it."

They reached her car, and after she'd unlocked her door, he opened it.

But he still didn't release her hand. Instead he used it to swing her around into his arms, where he kissed her again so soundly that it left her slightly dazed.

"I'll get you the information about the auction," he said, his voice deep and clearly under the influence of the same emotions that were making her knees weak.

Livi nodded.

He took his arms from around her, and when he did, it was more disappointing than she'd anticipated. And her knees really were a little wobbly without him, so she got behind the wheel of her car, fighting against what everything in her was crying out for—to be back in his arms, kissing him...

"Drive safe," Callan commanded, before he closed her door.

She nodded, stealing one last glance at him, wondering how it was possible that she was feeling what she was and wanting what she was when he wasn't Patrick, and when there weren't any of the other factors or elements that had brought her to his hotel room that night in Hawaii.

Then Callan smiled at her in a way that made her think he was almost as confused by what was happening as she was, before he moved so she could back out of the parking spot.

But even as confused as she was, she still drove home thinking about how amazingly good it had felt to have his hands on her.

And how much she wanted to have them on her again...

Chapter Nine

After telling herself all week that she should, Livi did not cancel with Callan on Saturday night.

In hopes of getting some control over herself, she'd spent the week avoiding him. She'd seen Greta only in public places like the mall and the ice-cream shop, before delivering the little girl to the condo's front door and ducking out in a hurry.

But by Saturday Livi wanted to see Callan all the more and there was just no way she could give up that opportunity.

So she spent the entire day getting ready.

And thinking while she was waxed and manicured and pedicured. While she had her hair trimmed and styled so that it was curlier than she ordinarily wore it. While she had her eyebrows done. While she even had China—the makeup artist who was best friends with her brother Dylan's fiancée, Abby—do her makeup.

Thinking and thinking and thinking...

On Friday night Livi had gathered her entire family together to tell them she was pregnant.

Everyone had had the same reaction as Jani and Lindie: shock that quickly turned to support and vows to be there for her any time of the day or night.

But Livi had also been in line for some pressure from her cousin Beau and her other triplet, Lang.

They both had strong opinions about whether or not Livi should tell Callan she was pregnant. Lang hadn't known about his own son, Carter, until the boy was two, and it had shaken up his entire life.

Thanks to machinations by their great-grandfather H.J., Beau had been left in the dark about having gotten his teenage sweetheart pregnant, and learned about it only a few months ago, when the two of them had met again. The belated news had come as a terrible blow to him, compounded by the fact that the baby had been lost in a miscarriage that the mother had suffered alone.

Livi had made the same points against telling Callan that she'd made with Jani and Lindie. But her male cousin and her brother had been insistent.

"Do it anyway," Beau had commanded, discounting everything she'd said. "The longer you wait, the harder it'll be, and it has to be done."

Livi realized that her cousin was right about one thing—the longer she waited, the more difficult it was. Even now, she felt guilty over the fact that while it felt as if they were not only getting to know each other, but actually getting close, she was keeping this enormous secret from Callan. She was willing to be intimate with him in a way that she'd been with only one other man in her life, but she wasn't being honest with him.

But not even worrying and fretting and agonizing about that had gotten her any closer to a decision. Because whenever Livi tried to think about what she should say to Callan, her mind wandered instead to how much she wanted him.

She hadn't been able to eat, to sleep, to focus or concentrate on work, because no matter what she did, she kept finding herself remembering him kissing her, touching her, or making love to her once upon a time in Hawaii.

It was chemistry, she'd finally concluded. Chemistry at its most extreme. In Hawaii and again now. And that chemistry dominated everything else.

Maybe Livi just had to let nature run its course. To get wanting him out of her system before she would ever be able to think straight.

So no, she hadn't canceled with Callan for tonight. And she'd given herself a temporary pass on making her decision about telling him she was pregnant, too.

The only decision she'd made was to dedicate tonight to whatever it took to resolve their chemistry.

When her day of beautification was done late that afternoon, she went home to put on the dress she'd bought for the occasion—a little black, knee-length cocktail dress with a lace overlay on the V-neck bodice that topped a full faille skirt.

Sheer black, thigh-high hose, a pair of strappy three-inch-high heels and a small black satin clutch completed the outfit only minutes before her doorbell rang.

Anticipation of seeing Callan again erupted an almost overwhelming rush of excitement through her. But she forced herself to walk at a moderate speed to the door.

He looked so good that her first glimpse of him took her breath away.

He was wearing a black, slim-cut, shawl-collar tuxedo with a crisp white shirt, and rather than a bow tie, a solid black silk tie that matched the tuxedo to a T.

His hair was in its usual tidy disarray, his face was clean-shaven and he smelled of that cologne she liked so much. Livi wasn't sure whether he really did look even better than normal or if it was just that she was starving for the sight of him. But one way or another she was bowled over.

"Wow!" he said, after giving her the same kind of once-over she'd given him. "Aren't you...wow. I don't want to take you out and share you."

"You clean up pretty well yourself," she countered.

He didn't acknowledge that, continuing to stare at her for another moment before he jolted out of his reverie and said, "We should get going—they won't start anything until I get there."

Livi had her clutch bag in her hand and held it up. "I'm ready if you are."

Ready and too, too eager to be with him again.

But as the evening progressed Livi had her own regrets about the necessity of sharing Callan, because she had to do so much of it.

Although there was staff galore to run the event, as sponsor and host, he was in big demand by everyone attending the function. He couldn't be rude to the legion of guests who wanted to say hello and chat, who barely left them a moment for a few bites of food and who waylaid them every time they headed for the dance floor that they never managed to reach.

All through it Livi stood by his Callan's side and per-severed, chafing over not having him to herself.

It was eleven o'clock before the results of the auc-tion had been tallied and announcements were made by the emcee, along with instructions on how the winners could check out.

Livi won a bid on a mural painting service that she thought Greta would like to use to make her bedroom at Callan's condo more kid-like—having okayed it with him before placing the bid.

Callan won a limited-edition bottle of scotch, and once they'd paid and he had his scotch and Livi had the receipt and information about how to redeem her pur-chase, he asked if she wanted to stay or if they could begin their exit.

She voted for the latter, but it was still midnight be-fore they made it out the door and back into Callan's sleek silver sports car.

"Thanks for being my wingman—or is that wing-woman—tonight. It was nice not having to do all that on my own," he said as he headed for Livi's house.

"Sure."

"You're good at it, too—all the people and small talk…. I've never cared for that stuff."

"You and John Sr. have that in common," Livi ob-served. "But I couldn't tell that you don't like it—you hid it very well."

Callan cast her a mischievous smile. "All an act," he confided.

She watched him as he pulled off his tie, then unfas-tened the top button of his shirt and stretched his neck as if to get the kinks out. And she fought the inclination to reach over and rub those kinks out for him.

"I was hoping we might have a few minutes to ourselves—to dance or just to talk—and maybe I could make the event a little more fun for you," he said. "But there was no chance, was there? I'm sorry for that."

Me, too...

"It's okay. I'm not a newbie at things like this—we go to them or throw them ourselves all the time. I knew what I was in for," she assured him, keeping her thoughts to herself.

He gave her a sidelong glance. "And you came anyway...just for me?" he asked, wiggling his eyebrows comically.

Yes, for him. Because of him. But Livi wasn't going to tell him that, so she said, "For the cause."

He just grinned, as if he knew her real answer.

Then he said, "So where were you all week? I know you saw Greta almost every day, but you made yourself scarce otherwise."

"Busy week," she lied. "But I heard that you were home to have dinner with Greta and the Tellers every single night."

"Told you I'd make more of an effort, didn't I?"

"And you came through."

"You didn't think I would," he accused, as they reached her house.

"I hoped for the best," she said, just before he pulled into her driveway and turned off the engine.

He got out to come around to her side, and as he did, Livi took a deep breath.

Was she going to ask him in?

On the previous Saturday night, she'd wished she had. But it was a big step to actually invite that man into the home she'd shared with Patrick. Especially when she considered what could happen when she did.

Not that it *had* to...

She could stop it from getting to the bedroom if anything about that didn't feel right, she told herself.

And knowing that she had the option was enough to get her out of the car and to her house. Where Callan did accept her invitation.

"How was it—going home to a family, to dinner with everyone, every night?" she asked as she closed the door behind them and set her purse on a table nearby.

"I think things went pretty well," he answered, following her into the living room, where she kicked off her shoes.

As his hostess, she knew she should offer him something to drink, but she didn't want the wine issue she'd skirted around at the auction to come up again. She'd ordered only pomegranate juice with a twist of lime and explained it away by saying that she liked to keep her wits about her when there would be names to remember.

But now she wouldn't have that excuse, so she merely sat on the couch, tucking her legs under her.

If Callan noticed the lack of etiquette he didn't show it and instead made himself at home by removing his tuxedo jacket and tossing it across the back of an easy chair before joining her on the sofa.

He sat nearby, angled toward her, his elbow hooked atop the cushions behind them, relaxed but intimate.

And even though Patrick crossed Livi's mind, it was only in realizing that nothing about having Callan there like that alarmed her. She wasn't thinking that Callan was in Patrick's place. She was just somehow comfortable with the fact that she was there, like that, with Callan.

Who she was still drinking in the sight of...

"Did you and John Sr. talk over dinner or are the two of you still doing that thing you do—talking to Greta and Maeve and Kinsey and never really to each other?"

"We did a little better. Monday night we exchanged a few words about going car shopping, which we did on Tuesday. I got him an SUV that feels like a truck to him, he said. Then one night he said it ran well. Another night he told me he was picking up Louie so Louie could show him some shortcuts and easy routes to use around town. And after that I asked him how it went and he said fine."

Livi laughed. "Let me guess—none of that is a brief summary of longer conversations. They're the totality of the few words you said to each other before you both went back to not talking, or only talking to everyone else."

Callan laughed, too. "Well, yeah..." he admitted. "But John Sr. went all week without saying anything bad about me under his breath—that's something. And he even said it felt good to have a way to get out around here—I took that as a thank-you for the car. Oh, and Thursday night he told me he'd do some grocery shopping on Friday, and asked if I needed anything..."

"That's pretty big, actually," Livi commented.

"So I don't think we're doing too badly. We're not BFFs yet or anything, but we aren't at each other's throats, either."

She smiled at his BFF remark. She doubted that term had been in his vocabulary before taking in a nine-year-old girl. "And Greta has been talking your ear off?"

"I don't know how you know that, but yeah," he said, sounding somewhat worn-out by the little girl.

"That's the way she is with people she likes," Livi

explained. "It's great, though, that she's talking to you. That's how you build your relationship with her, too. You should enjoy it while it lasts, because in a few years she'll be a teenager and she'll clam up."

"How soon is that?" he asked hopefully, clearly teasing.

"And how about Maeve?" Livi asked. "Kinsey had her trying to stand on that leg when I brought Greta home yesterday."

"Yeah, Kinsey switched her over to a home health care service here. They sent a doctor to admit her and the new doc thought she could start doing that a little. Seemed to go okay. Kinsey's been great helping her through it, coming in even earlier, staying later."

Livi had a brief flash of that jealousy she'd felt thinking about Callan and the pretty nurse. But she reminded herself that there was nothing going on between them. Also, it was her own choice to make herself scarce this past week. Greta had tried to persuade her to stay for dinner every night and she'd declined, so if Callan had spent more time with the nurse than with her, it was Livi's own fault.

"So are we all caught up?" Callan asked then.

She laughed once more. "Why? Do you have something else you want to talk about?"

"You."

"Me? What's there to say about me?"

He straightened his arm along the back of the couch, catching a strand of her hair and letting it wind around his finger. "Now that I know more, there's something that's bothering me about Hawaii."

He paused, his frown making it clear that this was

troubling him. "Did I sort of take your virginity without knowing that's what I was doing?"

"My virginity? I was married, remember? You definitely didn't take my virginity."

"I don't know..." he mused, unconvinced. "It was a first—a couple of pretty big firsts, actually. The first time after you lost your husband. The first time ever with someone who *wasn't* Patrick. And I didn't know."

"Would it have changed anything if you had?" Livi asked.

He chuckled wryly. "Fair question. I don't know. I guess I would have been a lot more careful to make sure you knew what you were doing, and wouldn't hate yourself—and me—in the morning."

She smiled sheepishly. "I have to admit that there was some of that," she confessed.

"So I'm kind of worried about what it all means for you now. You were drinking in Hawaii, but since then I haven't seen you drink so much as a glass of wine. Did you swear off alcohol because of what it led to in Hawaii? Is that part of the 'keeping your wits about you' thing you said tonight?"

"No. After Hawaii it's probably not easy for you to believe, but I've never been a big drinker." Which was true.

"It isn't because you're afraid, and staying supersober to ward me off? I'm wondering if I've been pushing you, if I have a lot to apologize for—last Sunday night included. If maybe that's why you made yourself scarce this past week..."

Apparently he'd done a lot of thinking—and worrying—himself.

Livi shook her head firmly. "No, that's not true," she

said. "There's nothing for you to apologize for." Although she liked that he had enough conscience to be concerned.

"Yes, I was drinking in Hawaii," she said then. "And I'm not sure I would have done what we did if I hadn't been. But that isn't on you—it's on me. And last Sunday night..." She shook her head again and tried to repress the surge of desire at the memories.

But she wasn't sure how to finish that sentence now that she'd started it, and all she could come up with was, "It takes two."

"So you aren't looking at me and seeing a wolf in sheep's clothing who's been preying on you?"

Oh, she was looking at him all right. And seeing a hot hunk in well-tailored clothing. That she wanted to rip off him.

But she said, "No, I don't think you're a wolf in sheep's clothing. That's actually what you've been worried *I* am, isn't it?"

He laughed. "Yeah, I guess that does fit what I think Mandy would be worried about with you, doesn't it?" He paused again, then returned to what he'd been saying. "I just want to make sure that we're okay. That I can think back on Hawaii and not feel like some kind of slimebag who took advantage of you."

"Nothing about you makes me think for a minute that you're a slimebag," Livi said honestly. "I mean, I did, when I thought you'd just run out that night in Hawaii. But now I know what happened, and leaving the way you did is understandable. Anyone would have done the same thing."

"So is it okay if I do this?"

He kissed her, just a simple meeting of their mouths with gentle care. But soon his lips parted and drew hers along, and that kiss became potent enough to wipe her thoughts clean.

Then he stopped, and she said, "Oh, you're good at that…"

"Does that mean it's okay?"

She offered herself the option to say no. Knowing that he would accept that answer and that likely everything would halt between them—the times alone when they got to talk. The kissing. The touching. Everything. And they would become nothing but the passing acquaintances she kept telling herself they *should* be.

She could go back to just being Patrick's widow.

But in that moment, even in that house that had belonged to her and Patrick, even still loving Patrick and cherishing everything he'd been to her, Livi knew with sudden but absolute certainty that living in the past was no longer what she wanted.

But another night with Callan was.

And maybe if she allowed herself that, it *would* get it out of her system, so she could think more clearly about whether or not to tell him she was pregnant with his child.

"It is okay," she heard herself whisper, looking into those dark eyes of his. "I'm not really sure why it is, but it is."

He searched her face as if to read in her expression whether or not he could trust what she was saying.

Then he said, "I hope so. Because I don't think I've ever wanted anything as much as I want you, right now."

He brought his other hand to her cheek and guided her into a second kiss that was instantly more heated than the first, instantly more intimate. Lips parted, and tongues sought each other out with an all new fervor.

No more fiddling with her hair; Callan wrapped his arm around her instead. He pulled her closer while his kiss increased in power and passion, fueling every hunger and need she'd been fighting this past week. The kiss was so intense it wiped away all thoughts and left her awash in nothing but sensations and desires and excitement.

Her hands were in his hair, down his neck, across his broad shoulders and then splayed on his back, as she again imagined tearing off his clothes.

But now there was nothing to stop her.

So she brought her hands around to his front, where she began to unbutton his shirt, not pausing until she'd pulled the tails out of his tuxedo pants and had the whole thing laid open.

Then her palms traveled from impressively honed pectorals up and over his shoulders to push his shirt as far off as she could get it.

She felt him smile even as they kissed, and he let go of her so that she could take his shirt completely off.

When she'd done that, he reached around her to unzip her dress.

Livi was just as thrilled with the prospect of getting rid of her own clothes as she was with getting rid of his. But maybe not in her living room.

So before he got her zipper down too far she ended their kiss.

And Callan yanked his hands away and held them up and out to the side as if he was being arrested. "Changed your mind?"

She laughed. "Yes," she said out of pure orneriness, before she took one of those upraised hands and tugged him with her off the couch and to the stairs toward her bedroom.

"You're sure?" he asked, when they got there.

She was and she told him so, leaving him while she went to her nightstand and turned on the small lamp there so that a faint golden glow lit the room.

She'd wanted total darkness in Hawaii. She didn't want it tonight. And now that she could truly see Callan, shirtless in the lamplight, she realized what she'd missed.

And she had missed out, all right! Because it wasn't only his great hair and strikingly handsome face that were stare-worthy, so was his torso—sculpted and chiseled and buff.

When he bent over to take off his shoes and socks, she was hoping that his pants would be the next to go.

But all he did was unfasten his waistband, whetting her appetite, as he glanced around at the room she'd refurnished and redecorated a year ago to make it completely her own.

She didn't know if Callan was looking for ghosts, but that was the impression she had. He wouldn't find one, if he was. Packing away all Patrick's things had been one of the moving-on projects Jani and Lindie had talked her into. And although Livi kept several framed photographs of Patrick on her nightstand, she'd put them in the drawer earlier tonight when she'd been getting ready. Just in case this happened.

"Have *you* changed *your* mind?" she asked, when he continued scanning the room.

His espresso-colored eyes settled on her and he grinned. "Not on your life."

He closed the distance between them in three steps and pulled her to him with caveman force, claiming her mouth again in a kiss that was all primitive hunger while he found her zipper once more, wasting no time opening it.

He left her dress in place, though, only snaking his big hands inside, massaging her back and making her ever more pliable as his mouth plundered hers.

Her breasts had ached all week long for more of his touch, and the longer he denied them, the greater the ache became.

Livi raised her hands to his pecs and demonstrated what she wanted even as she reveled in the feel of him. She hadn't realized just how blurred and blunted by alcohol everything in Hawaii had been. Because now everything was sharper and clearer and so, so much better. So much more real. Now every sense, every awareness and response, every nerve ending seemed finely tuned and turned on.

Callan brought his hands up and over her shoulders, and down came her dress, to the beginning swell of her breasts.

But it was quite a swell. Her black lace demi-cup bra barely fit breasts that pregnancy had apparently increased a size.

He deserted her mouth to kiss the side of her neck, the tip of her shoulder and then those breasts where they spilled out of their confines.

He placed the lightest of kisses there, and still it felt so good that her breath caught in her throat.

And that was nothing compared to what followed.

He moved her dress down farther until it drifted to the floor around her ankles. And once it was gone he nuzzled one of the bra's cups below her breast and took that breast into his mouth.

Another breath caught, and as she sighed it out she heard herself moan, "Oh, you're good at that, too..." because, oh, he was! And coupled with the pregnancy benefit of heightened sensitivity that she'd discovered on Sunday night, it was almost enough to make her lose her mind. It was most certainly enough to give her the courage to reach for the zipper of his tuxedo pants, easing down those well-tailored trousers and the boxers he had on underneath.

He stepped free of them, ended the delights at her breast and scooped her up into his arms to swing her onto the bed, before returning to his slacks to extract a condom from his pocket.

But Livi barely noticed anything but him. Gloriously naked and magnificent and so clearly wanting her.

Then he came to the foot of the bed and with a devilish half smile began to slowly roll her thigh-high nylons off—first one, then the other—getting his own fill of studying her body before he crawled onto the mattress.

He again captured her mouth, ravishing it while his hand reached the breast that was still exposed above the bra's cup, tormenting her diamond-hard nipple for a while before he reached around and unfastened her bra, taking it off so both breasts were free.

His mouth went from hers to her breasts again, giving them both equal time while that big hand of his trailed down her stomach and dipped between her legs.

Oh. Things were more sensitive there, too. When he slipped a finger into her, Livi's back came up off the bed and a high-pitched little groan accompanied it.

She wasn't going to be able to contain herself. The pleasure was too keen already and building in her by the minute.

So she reached between *his* legs, encasing him, sliding from base to tip and back again, driving him as mad as he was driving her, bringing him to the same brink.

That was when he paused to make quick work of putting on the condom he didn't know they didn't need. Then he did what everything in her was screaming for—he repositioned himself over and above her and came into her in one lithe move.

Never had Livi felt quite what she did then, as he began to thrust slowly in and out, picking up speed as he went. She kept up, rising to meet him and then drawing just enough away to tempt him back again.

Her hands were again pressed flat to his back, her fingers digging into him, holding tight as he took her on a wild ride that just got faster and faster and more intense as it went.

Until bliss engulfed her and him at once, wrapping them in a whirlwind of primal, exquisite euphoria that suspended everything for that one endless moment, unmatched by anything that had come before.

When it passed, the sensations depleted her so totally that she nearly collapsed into Callan's waiting embrace, not having realized that somewhere along the way they'd come to their sides and were not only joined but entwined together. It was impossible to know where one of them began and the other left off.

There were a few moments of settling. Of calming. Of her pulse slowing back to normal, her breathing doing the same. Of wilting against the big, strong, muscular body wrapped around her.

"Amazing," Callan whispered in awe.

She couldn't refute or improve upon that, so merely murmured in response.

"Are you okay?" he asked.

"Ohh...yeah. Are you?"

He gave a throaty, replete laugh. "Ohh...yeah," he parroted back. Then, holding her a little tighter, he said, "Can I stay?"

It hadn't occurred to her that he might not. "I thought you would."

"Great," he said with an exhausted sigh, fully relaxing. He got up to dispose of the condom, and then settled back in beside her. She felt him tense as something else seemed to occur to him.

"The whole night," he added, as if he suddenly needed that specified. "I want to be here the whole night."

"I wasn't planning to kick you out as payback. Or disappear myself, to teach you a lesson," she said with a small laugh.

"I'd have it coming."

"The whole night," she confirmed sleepily.

Maybe he'd realized she was about to drift off, because he said, "Can I wake you up after we nap a little?"

She moaned, liking that idea a lot. "You can."

"Good," he said, resting his head atop hers as she nestled into his chest. He held her close as she felt him falling asleep.

And as she drew nearer and nearer to slumber herself, she suddenly had a moment of crystal clarity.

A moment in which she knew exactly what she had to do.

She had to tell him she was pregnant.

Chapter Ten

"Are you okay?"

This time Callan wasn't asking the question after a round of runaway lovemaking. He was asking it through Livi's bathroom door, after morning sickness had sent her running for the second time.

Sure, she'd decided to tell him she was pregnant, but she'd wanted to be able to choose the right moment, the right setting. Right now, just after he'd listened to her throwing up, really wasn't it. But she didn't seem to have much of a choice.

They'd had an incredible night together. But fearing what happened every morning, after their third round of lovemaking at nearly 5:00 a.m. on Sunday, Livi had tried to persuade Callan that he should go home before the Tellers or Greta got up and realized he'd been out all night.

He'd listened to and acted on all her other suggestions for this role he'd taken with his makeshift family. But not that one. And lying warmly, snugly, in his arms had felt so good she hadn't insisted.

Instead she'd fallen asleep, willing herself to wake up feeling fine. But just like every other day, at nearly the stroke of seven, nausea woke her up.

The everyday illness had settled into a pattern, though. After the second upchuck she knew she would be able to hold down a few soda crackers, and would be left with an upset stomach for only the next couple hours.

So she called back to Callan in answer, "I'm okay. I just need a minute."

Then she brushed her teeth, rinsed with mouthwash, pressed a cool cloth to her face, ran a brush through her hair and wrapped herself in her robe before going out.

To face the music.

"You don't look okay," Callan greeted her, frowning, sounding caring and compassionate.

Sick or not, Livi smiled weakly and wondered how he could look as good as he did right out of bed with his hair tousled and a scruff of beard shadowing his face. He'd pulled on his tuxedo pants and the shirt he'd worn the night before—left untucked and unbuttoned so a strip of his glorious chest and rock-hard abs peeked out, distracting her.

But right now she had to focus, to respond to his comment on her appearance. "Thanks," she said facetiously.

"You're beautiful, but you don't look well," he amended. "What's going on? Do you think you have the flu? This isn't some kind of extreme morning-after regret, is it?"

Livi laughed slightly. He'd clearly meant it as a joke,

but sounded a little worried that there might be a grain of truth to it.

She went to her nightstand and took a sleeve of crackers from the drawer. Turning back to Callan, she offered him one.

"Crackers? In here? Now?" he said, after he'd declined the offer.

Livi took a few for herself and returned the sleeve to her drawer. Apparently his ex-wife hadn't suffered morning sickness—or maybe Callan just hadn't been around enough during the pregnancy to know about the remedy that Livi's obstetrician had recommended.

"Keeping crackers in here and eating them first thing is not something I've done until lately," she said, thinking that waiting until now to tell him about the baby really did make it even harder to do.

But she knew she had to.

So she said, "The nausea *is* a morning-after thing, but not from last night." Taking her crackers, she went to sit on the end of her rumpled bed before she nibbled on one.

Callan came to stand in front of her, frowning down at her. "What does that mean?"

"I honestly didn't know whether to tell you this or not," she said with a sigh.

Then she took a steeling breath, shored up her courage, met his eyes with hers and said, "Remember that broken condom in Hawaii?"

She watched the color drain from his face. But he seemed at a loss for words as he just stood there, staring at her.

On the off chance that he might not have understood, she made it very clear. "I'm pregnant, Callan. A little over two months now."

"Pregnant…" he echoed, sounding thunderstruck.

Livi nodded. "I did a home test and then saw my doctor to confirm it." She told him her due date and saw him swallow.

The expression on his face wasn't merely a frown anymore. It had darkened into something more serious, something that reminded her of a gathering storm.

"Two and a half months," he repeated. "You've known for that long. You knew through this…" He pointed with a raise of his chin to the bed they'd shared all night.

"At first, I just couldn't face that it might be true. I've only *really* known and been able to accept it for a couple of weeks."

"A couple of weeks." More parroting, but with some outrage around the fringes. "The same couple of weeks we've been seeing each other, talking to each other… But again—we got all the way here last night without you telling me?"

He was definitely not happy.

But before Livi had the chance to say anything else, something seemed to dawn on him and make his ire grow. "Oh, my God, this is it, isn't it? This is really why you came around wanting contact with Greta! It wasn't to make up for what your family did to hers. That was just the cover story. You came to get to me. Mandy was right about you Camdens!"

Livi hadn't expected that.

"No! I was in Northbridge to see Greta. I knew she had a guardian, but I didn't have any idea it was you. I didn't even know your last name. And everything to do with Greta is completely separate from you or any of this—it was from the start, it is now and it will be from here on, regardless of what's going on between you and me. I was completely stunned to see you in Northbridge."

"Come on," he said skeptically. "Admit it—you realized you were pregnant and did something to figure out who the guy you'd spent the night with in Hawaii was, didn't you? You knew," he said accusingly. "You just put on a show when I walked into the Tellers' house that day. I'll bet your cousin Seth gave you the heads-up that the guy you were looking for was right there under his nose, and you all hatched some plot to get to me through Greta."

"That's not true," Livi insisted.

Callan huffed in disgust. "And just when I honestly thought the Camdens might be all right, after all. That Mandy would have been wrong to think of you in the same category with the Camdens who screwed over her dad. Just when I actually thought maybe you could be trusted..."

"There's no conspiracy, Callan. My family didn't even know until this past week—I told them Friday night, and Lang and Beau lectured me then, saying I needed to tell you. They were talking from your perspective, and I guess it sank in that you would *want* to know. But what you're saying now doesn't even make sense. Why would I need to use Greta to get to you? If I had known—or found out—who you are, what was there to keep me from just going where you live or work? What possible purpose could there be for doing it through Greta?"

Callan didn't have an answer for that, but he wasn't readily conceding to her reasoning, either. He still just stood there, his dark eyes boring into her suspiciously.

"Maybe I shouldn't have told you," she said then, thinking out loud.

But that just seemed to send him off onto a new path of anger. "I should have been the first to know—after you," he declared. "I sure as hell shouldn't have been the last. But then the end of the line does seem to be where I always am in these things."

Livi knew he was referring to his ex-wife's deception. "You aren't at the end of the line. My brother didn't know he was a father until Carter was two, and my cousin didn't find out that he'd gotten his high school girlfriend pregnant until just recently."

"Is that supposed to make this better?"

Livi's stomach lurched and she spent a moment waiting to see if she needed a third run for the bathroom, after all.

Only when she knew she was going to avoid throwing up again did she take a deep breath and say, "I know you already have your hands full with Greta and the Tellers. I wasn't sure you could handle more on top of it, especially when family is not really your thing. Not that you aren't trying, but still…" She took another small bite of the corner of a cracker to keep back the bile that seemed to be building again.

Then she said, "But Beau and Lang convinced me that you *could* handle it—that you *had* to know. So now you do. But if you want, you can just forget it."

"Forget it?" Callan shouted.

"I have a good support system," she went on, trying to reassure him. "I won't be alone in this. I don't need anything financially. If you don't want to see me again, then I can make that happen. We didn't see each other all last week. I can go on meeting with Greta the way I did, and you can go on about your business as if you were none the wiser. You can just concentrate on deal-

ing with what you already have on your plate. It'll be
fine. I'm giving you knowledge, not another obligation."

He released a huff filled with a combination of astonishment and fury and frustration and confusion—
so many things that Livi went on to say, "I know this is
huge. And believe me, it took me a *long* time to face it,
to admit even to myself that it's happening. You need
some time with it… I just want you to know up front
that there are no expectations of you—"

He pressed all ten fingertips to his head as if to keep
it from exploding, his eyes closed.

Livi had the sense that everything she was saying
was making it worse—but she didn't know how to make
things right.

Then he opened his eyes, took his hands away from
his head and held them palms out. "I do have to wrap
my head around this," he said, as if he didn't trust himself to say any more.

He started to button his shirt faster than she'd ever
seen it done.

"Do you need me for anything right now?" he asked
as he did. "Is there something I can do for the…sickness?
Make you tea? Get you water? Something?"

It was the most irate offer to do something nice that
she'd ever heard.

Livi shook her head. "I'm fine. I do this every morning. It passes."

And why on earth did she feel as if she was about to
cry? Of course she hadn't fooled herself into believing
that he would embrace this news and be thrilled with it
the way Patrick would have been.

But rage and accusations, followed by Callan not
being able to get away fast enough? Not only was it all

a bad reaction, it was also an awful ending to the night they'd spent together. She wished they were still lying in bed, that she was wrapped in his arms, both of them just savoring the afterglow. But that couldn't happen now. Maybe it would never happen again. Instead she was sick and he was fuming.

They really didn't do the morning-after thing very well...

"You're sure there's nothing you need?" he asked.

"Positive," she said, struggling to keep her voice from cracking, to show him nothing but strength and proof that she could do this on her own.

"I need to think," he told her, as if he'd forgotten they'd already determined that.

She nodded and agreed. "You do."

She thought he would leave then. But for another moment he went on standing there, looking cross and confused and frustrated and helpless all at once. She didn't know why he didn't just go.

"It's okay," she assured him, sounding impatient in her attempt to conceal her own bewildering emotions. "Leave!"

She wasn't sure why that had come out so harsh, but it had.

Callan snatched up what remained of his discarded clothes and went to her bedroom door. But even once he reached it, with his hand on the knob, he didn't rush out.

Instead he paused there, looking back in her direction, but at the floor.

"You were right to tell me. But not to wait until now."

Livi didn't say anything. She couldn't. Not with a throat full of tears.

After a moment of only silence from her, Callan opened

the door and went out. Moments later, she heard her front door open and slam shut.

And that was when she recognized the feelings she was having.

Feelings she hadn't ever expected to have again.

The same feelings she'd had when it had sunk in that she'd lost Patrick.

Only this time they were all about Callan.

Chapter Eleven

"What am I doing?" Callan shouted, when he emerged from his fog and registered where he was—at his office building. But it was Sunday morning and when he'd stormed out of Livi's house it had been with the intention of going home.

Cursing, he hit his steering wheel with the heels of his hands as if the car was to blame for taking him to the wrong place. But the truth was he had so much on his mind that he'd driven without thinking.

Disgusted with himself, he slammed the gearshift into reverse and backed out of his parking spot to try again.

But his mind detoured once more, back to Livi and what she'd just told him.

She was pregnant.

Another rug pulled out from under him, with another pregnancy.

Maybe this baby wasn't his, either.

"You didn't even ask that, you idiot!" he said to himself.

Considering that he'd already had one woman try to pass off someone else's baby on him, that should have been his first question. But it had only just occurred to him.

Why was that? he wondered, as he pulled out of the parking garage and headed for his condominium.

Maybe it was because he didn't really doubt that he was the father.

The condom *had* broken, he reminded himself. Plus, everything he'd learned about Livi's past, about her and the kind of person she was, didn't leave him any doubts that he really had been the first man she'd been with since her husband's death.

"Yeah, but she could have come back from Hawaii and really cut loose," he argued with himself angrily.

But livid or not, he still knew that that wasn't Livi, either. She'd been so shocked that *anyone* had been able to shake her loyalty to her late soul mate. Spending the night with him in Hawaii had been way, way too monumental to her to have gone beyond that.

Until last night…

But he didn't want to think about last night. Last night had been mind-blowing, and remembering any part of it blunted the force of that bomb she'd dropped on him. And he didn't want it blunted. Not when he needed to see beyond the attraction between them to figure out how to deal with the fact that she was pregnant.

Pregnant, for God's sake.

And this time he was sure it was his.

Yet he somehow felt just as betrayed as he had when he'd found out his assistant had fathered his wife's baby.

How come? Callan asked himself. One baby was his, one wasn't, and those weren't the same...

But he'd still been left in the dark both times. He'd still felt played both times.

Played by Elly, who had been his wife and should have been loyal to him.

Played by Livi, who he'd just started to drop his guard with. Who he'd just started to trust. To let in the way he'd let in Mandy and J.J. And Elly. Just so he could be as blindsided by Livi as he had been by his ex-wife.

That was why the betrayal felt the same.

There was a part of him that wanted to push Livi away. To punish her. To protect himself. A part of him that wanted to just say to hell with her and everything to do with her! He didn't need another woman in his life who wasn't up-front with him!

But even as furious as he was, he couldn't forget that there was going to be a baby.

His baby.

And if that was the case, he couldn't say to hell with anything...

His condo was near his office, so it didn't take long to get home. This time when he parked, he turned off the engine and got out.

He was glad not to meet anyone as he stepped into the waiting elevator, then ferociously punched the button for his floor.

As the doors closed, he drew both hands through his hair, pulling hard on his scalp as if that might calm him down.

It didn't. And when he'd gotten off the elevator and

went across to his door, he jammed his key into the lock
with a vengeance.

He was just so damn mad! He'd actually been thinking that Livi was something special. That things with her
might have a chance of going somewhere.

Then she had to go and pull this!

He opened the door and went in, to find John Sr. already up and sitting at the island counter in his kitchen,
drinking a cup of coffee.

Great.

"Morning," Callan grumbled to the elderly man, barely
civil.

John Sr. gave him a once-over that took in the fact that
he was wearing the same clothes he'd had on last night.
But all his late best friend's father said was, "Morning."

Callan considered what to do in this situation.

What he wanted to do was just be alone.

But *that* wasn't going to happen.

On the other hand, he was an adult who sure as hell
shouldn't have to feel embarrassed or ashamed of having spent a night with a woman.

And he wasn't going to slink off to his bedroom as
if he was.

So he tried again to get some control over his temper,
tossed his tuxedo coat and tie over the arm of the sofa,
and joined the older man in the kitchen, where he poured
himself a cup of coffee.

Unfortunately, there were still too many emotions running through him—running him—and when he went to
stand at the island across from John Sr., the best Callan
could do was set his cup down, lean on his elbows and
hold his head.

"Your party didn't go well?" John Sr. asked.

"It went fine. Big success. Raised more money than ever before," he answered.

"Long night, though…" the elderly man said.

"Yeah."

"With Livi?"

Oh, the old man was pushing it.

But Callan wasn't a teenager under John Sr.'s roof now. He was a grown man, in his own home, and he was going to do whatever he damn well pleased without tiptoeing around it.

"Yeah," he said, intending to sound firm.

Instead it had come out with a mixture of the emotions cascading through him.

"I like that girl," John Sr. said.

"Yeah. Me, too." But there was still that edge of anger in the admission. He'd liked who he thought she was, yet he still wondered if she'd been playing him. It was true—there was no logical reason for her to try to get to him through Greta, but people weren't always logical when it came to getting what they wanted.

The other man ignored his tone. "She's a nice girl. Some in her family before her might have been bastards, but I don't think it's carried on in those folks now. Especially not in Livi. I think she only means well. She's been good for Greta. Good for Maeve and me, too—bendin' over backward for us same as Kinsey, only without any paycheck comin' her way."

The old man chose now *to get wordy?* Callan thought.

He nodded but didn't comment, loath to listen to anything at the moment.

"Wouldn't want to think the good in her is bein' overlooked," John Sr. said, as if finally making his point.

The point being, Callan thought, that John Sr. still

saw him as little more than a troublemaker who was doing Livi wrong.

But while his instinctive response was to get even more riled up, he also couldn't help thinking that in this situation Livi would tell him he had to have patience. That he had to resist the past roles, the past patterns. That he had to work on forging a new relationship with this man.

And somewhere in that, something else suddenly dawned on Callan.

Here, sitting in his kitchen, was someone who had been married to the same woman for decades. Someone who was committed to doing whatever it took to care for his ailing wife—even when it meant leaving the home and land he loved and had worked on his entire life, to live in the home of someone he'd never liked. And it crossed Callan's mind that maybe he should mine that a little.

So he pushed himself off the counter to stand up straight and look J.J.'s father in the eye.

"How do you do it?" he asked.

Bushy gray eyebrows arched over rheumy eyes. "How do I do what?"

"The whole marriage-relationship thing. How long have you and Maeve been together?"

"Oh, better 'n fifty years."

"So how does that work? Because…I don't know. I blew it once. I don't know what's going on now… Maybe I just don't get it. Every time I think things are good, I get knocked on my ass."

Once-strong shoulders shrugged. "No master plan I can give you. Knew from the minute I laid eyes on Maeve that I was a better man with her than without her. That

I was nothin' without her. Always loved her. Always wanted to be with her."

"And you'll do anything, go anywhere, swallow whatever you have to swallow to do it?"

"What do I have to swallow?"

Callan started to list all the enormous changes the man was accepting.

But as he got into it, John Sr. began to shake his head, and when Callan had finished, the elderly man said, "Means nothin' to me. Maeve's what means something. Greta. Whatever it takes to be with 'em is what it takes. Otherwise, no Maeve. No Greta. And that'd be worse than anything I can think of."

"Maeve never went about something the worst way she could have? Enough to piss you off no end?" Callan muttered.

The old man laughed. "Hell, yes, she has. So what? Pissed her off plenty, too. Means nothin' in the long run."

"No matter what? No matter how complicated it gets? No matter what might be in the way?"

"Guess it would depend how big what got in the way was. For us? Nothin' was ever too big, too complicated to where it meant more than keeping what we've got. Not even now, leavin' Northbridge."

Callan stared into his coffee cup, feeling John Sr.'s eyes on him, expecting this to turn at any moment, for the judgmental voice of his youth to sound again.

But instead, as John Sr. picked up his own cup and took it to the sink, the elderly man said, "Nothin' worth havin' comes easy, boy. Trick is figurin' out what's worth havin'—and what's not—before you know what you can *swallow* and what you can't."

Then he headed into the room he shared with Maeve and left Callan alone.

To stew.

Because he *was* still stewing. He couldn't move past how much he hated it that in all the time he and Livi had spent together—including the night they'd just had together—she'd known she was pregnant with his baby and he hadn't. That she'd kept something that big from him. That, for even one minute, she'd pulled the wool over his eyes.

He hated it!

He *hated* it!

He sighed.

But I don't hate her...

He leaned on the counter, held his head again and tried harder to cool off.

How much of what he was feeling was his own past haunting him? How much of his anger at Livi was really lingering outrage at being made a fool by Elly and Trent?

Some of it, Callan admitted.

And he also acknowledged that Livi had kept the news from him for only a couple weeks after a period of denial herself. That couldn't really compare to the six months his wife had let him believe that he was the father of her baby. At least there was no lie in what Livi had done; there was just a brief omission. And the first opportunity she'd had to tell him—that day at the Tellers' farm—she'd still been rightfully furious with him for abandoning her after their encounter. Would he really have expected her to trust him with news of her pregnancy right away after that?

So maybe calling it a betrayal was somewhat of an exaggeration...

He pushed up from the counter a second time and sighed away a large portion of his rage.

But that just made way for something else.

She'd said she was worried that he had too much on his plate for anything else—and she wasn't exactly wrong. There were so many elements that still made this whole thing overwhelming—work and Greta and the Tellers and learning how to be all he needed to be for so many people already. And now there would be another kid—his own kid—and Livi...

Livi...

Okay, yeah, just the thought of her now—without unreasonable irritation—had its way with him again.

So-o-o...what if there wasn't anything at stake here but *Livi?* he asked himself, thinking then of what John Sr. had said.

Is she my Maeve?

He and Livi were good together—there was no doubt about that. Great together, actually. In *and* out of bed. Their sexual chemistry was off the charts, but every other minute they were together was great, too. Talking to her seemed to put even the worst day right again. Just being with her was its own kind of refuge—like an island where chaos got sorted through and put in order. Where she helped guide him to better ways of handling problems that otherwise seemed insurmountable.

Like John Sr. had said about Maeve, Callan thought that he was a better man with Livi's help. And, yes, he wanted to be better *for* her, too—which was why he'd altered his work schedule last week to make sure that his job didn't get in the way of his relationships. His relationship with Livi included, because he'd expected to see her last week.

And when he hadn't? When night after night he'd gone home to dinner hoping she'd be there and she wasn't?

He'd felt a gaping hole where she should have been. Even surrounded by the Tellers and Greta and Kinsey, who all made for a much fuller house than he'd ever been used to. But still, without Livi, it had seemed empty to him. Drab and colorless. Lacking its most important part.

Because Livi *was* the most important part, he realized suddenly.

The way Maeve was for John Sr.

Livi was the first thing he thought about when he woke up in the morning. She was who he thought about in terms of everything—what he wore, what he ate, how he scheduled his day and—like this morning—even how he treated other people in his life.

She was who he wanted to be with every minute. Who he wanted to share every piece of news with.

Even today, when he'd been furious with her, he'd still found it hard to leave her.

So she *was* his Maeve...

But thinking that brought Callan back around to the rest—to having Maeve and John Sr. and Greta already in his life, already his responsibility in ways that demanded more of him than he'd thought they would.

It brought him back around to the struggles he was already having balancing work with commitments at home.

It brought him back around to the whole complicated mess that also included his lost friend, who would go ballistic at the idea of a Camden in the life of her daughter.

It brought him back around to the late husband Livi idolized.

And now there would be a baby, too?

Callan leaned over the counter yet again to put his head in his hands.

That was a lot.

But just as John Sr. had decided it was worth anything to him to have Maeve, Callan realized that it was worth anything to him to have Livi. Livi and their baby.

More work, more adjustments, more relationships for him to figure out. But it was still all worth it.

Because otherwise there was no Livi.

And John Sr. was right—nothing was as bad as that.

For a moment Callan felt the weight of everything on his shoulders. Of even more to come with a baby on the way. But somehow feeling that weight and thinking about having Livi to help him with it suddenly made it all seem workable.

"Here's how it is, Mandy," he whispered to the memory of his friend. "You're gonna have to trust me that Livi is different than the Camdens who sank your dad. You're gonna have to trust me that it's not only good to have her around Greta, but that Livi makes me better at being your daughter's guardian."

And in thinking about his late friends, he also suddenly knew that Livi gave him what Mandy and J.J. had had.

Elly hadn't—there had never been the kind of closeness that Mandy and J.J. shared, the bond, the connection.

But with Livi it was all there. That and so much more.

Feelings that were deeper and stronger.

He loved her. With a power and a passion that he'd never known was in him.

"And I walked out on her again..." he groaned when that occurred to him. "After accusing her of some pretty awful things." He wished now that he hadn't done that. And wondered how much damage it might have caused.

Especially when he recalled her telling him pretty bitterly to leave...

Yeah, that wasn't good, he thought.

But no matter how things had been left between them, he wanted her, loved her, too much to let anything get in their way.

And he wanted her too much to let any more time go by without telling her that.

Chapter Twelve

Weeks of morning sickness had taught Livi showers helped. So after an hour of crying and fretting about what had happened with Callan—and feeling even worse than usual—she called upon what little energy and strength she had, and went into the bathroom to shower and shampoo her hair.

The spray of water washed the tears away, but couldn't stop them from falling. The last thing she wanted to do was go to her grandmother's house that evening for Sunday dinner with red puffy eyes and a swollen face. So once she turned her shower off, she put every effort into turning off her own waterworks, too. But her sadness wasn't as easily stifled.

What would have happened if she'd told Callan as soon as they'd met again in Northbridge? She couldn't help wondering.

But *she* hadn't even been able to accept it then; she hadn't even bought the home pregnancy test until after that Sunday when they'd met again at the Tellers' and she hadn't taken it until after that. And she'd still thought that he'd ditched her in Hawaii. Even once he'd told her the truth, she'd needed time to adjust her thinking and accept what had happened.

Had she handled everything perfectly? No. But it wasn't as if any of this had been easy. It wasn't as if she had any experience with this.

So what if she'd bided her time a little?

So what if she'd taken a misstep by not telling him the second she'd stopped denying it herself?

It wasn't as if *that* much time had gone by before she *had* told him. It wasn't as if he'd found out some other way.

What had she done that was so wrong? she wondered, beginning to find some solace in getting a little angry herself.

The condom had broken—that wasn't the fault of either of them, and the pregnancy was as big a shock to her as it was to Callan. What gave him the right to get on his high horse and ride out of here the way he had? Much less accuse her of using Greta in such an underhanded way. Didn't he know her better than that?

"Jerk," she muttered, as she wrapped a towel around herself and tucked the corner in to keep it in place.

Anger felt better than hurt, so she hung on to that as she blow-dried her hair. But when she took a look at herself in the bathroom mirror, she saw plainly that neither anger nor her shower had erased the evidence of her crying.

Maybe lying down for a while with a cold washcloth on her face would help.

She wet a fresh one, then took it with her into the bedroom.

Where Callan was sitting on the end of her bed as if he'd never left. He was even dressed the same way he had been in his tuxedo pants and shirt.

And maybe she was a little angrier than she thought. Because after the initial shock of finding him there, Livi threw the washcloth at him.

It hit him smack in the center of that broad chest.

"You left!" she said heatedly. "What are you doing here now and how did you get in?"

He put the wet washcloth on the bed beside him.

"I did leave," he replied. "But I guess I didn't lock the door behind me. And apparently you didn't notice and lock it yourself, because when you didn't answer the bell, I tried the door and it was open. Not really safe…"

"Well, since it was you who didn't lock it on your way out, thanks," she said facetiously. "Try to do better on your way out now."

"I'm not going anywhere," he said flatly. "I shouldn't have left before. I'm sorry for that."

Livi only raised her chin, not offering instant forgiveness or acceptance or encouragement. But not *dis*couraging him, either, merely waiting to see what came next.

"You hit a hot button, Livi," he said then, not sounding completely calm himself. "You have to understand— after six months of Elly making a fool out of me, *no* amount of time being kept in the dark about another pregnancy can sit well. But…" He sighed and seemed to let whatever remained of his anger release on that breath. "I know a couple of weeks isn't the huge deal that I made it into. And I shouldn't have done that. I definitely shouldn't have accused you of using Greta—I know you'd never do that. It's just that when my trust in you was shaken, I didn't know what to believe, so I defaulted back to my old opinion of Camdens. That wasn't fair to you, or to your family, who were nothing but kind and welcoming to me and the others when we came to dinner."

Livi did understand how any delay in finding out he was going to be a father could trigger old issues for him. And she understood why Callan might assume the worst of any Camden. But she still wasn't going to cave that easily, so she just raised her chin a notch higher.

"And you gotta admit, it's a shock to find out there's a baby on the way," he said, his tone, arched eyebrows and crinkled forehead all conveying that fact.

"For me, too," she reminded him curtly.

"I'm sure." There was empathy in his tone that pushed some of her own anger away.

But she still wasn't sure why he'd come back.

So she went on standing there, wrapped in her towel, trying to be strong when she felt anything but.

Callan stood up and met her gaze.

"I don't know if you know it or not," he said, "but you're an amazing person, Livi Camden. You're gorgeous and smart and wise and kind and generous and funny and fun to be with and…well, a million other things that make you seem like some kind of hidden treasure to me. You open my eyes and widen my horizons and make me better than I am. Better than I ever have been."

Was this a lead-in to him saying "so it's not you, it's me"?

"A lot went through my head when I left here," he

continued. "First and foremost that I didn't ask you if the baby is mine—"

Livi stiffened.

"But then I realized," he went on, "that the reason it didn't even occur to me is *because* you are all the things you are and there's really no way that baby *isn't* mine."

"It is," she felt compelled to say.

"I know. And I also know that trusting you enough not to doubt it—after Elly—is a very, very big thing. Almost as big a thing as the way I feel about you."

But he didn't go on to tell her how he felt about her. Instead he laid out for her all the things he'd thought about between when he'd left and when he'd returned, and the conclusions he'd come to.

Then, when he seemed to have covered all the bases, he took a step closer, peering down at her solemnly. "I know I'm just beginning to get the hang of parenthood, and you're right, I'm in the deep end with just about everything right now. But there's still no way I'm not going to be involved in my own kid's life. And I want it to be hand in hand with you. I want dealing with all that stuff that I'm in over my head with to be hand in hand with you, too—even if it does seem a little unfair to ask that of you."

Another step toward her, close enough that he could have reached out and touched her. But he didn't. And despite everything, she still wanted him to.

"I know I'm up against that two-halves-of-a-whole business about Patrick," Callan said. "I know you've gone through the last four years convinced that there couldn't be anyone else for you. But I think that if you just consider how good we are together, what we have when we're together…" He stalled. Then said, "I think together we make two halves of a new whole. A whole of our own. And maybe I'll never measure up, but I'm willing to spend my life working on it. If you'll let me..."

He paused again, looked more deeply into her eyes and said, "I love you, Livi. Believe it or not, John Sr. actually helped me weed through things this morning to realize that. And even if there wasn't a baby on board, I'd still be here telling you this and asking you to give me another chance."

Apparently he was taking a turn at shocking her. And she didn't know whether it was that shock that sent a noticeable shiver through her or if it came from still standing there naked but for a damp towel.

"I need to put something on," she said. Which might have been true. But she also needed a moment to herself, a moment to think.

Callan nodded once, his expression making it clear that he feared the worst and was waiting for the hammer to drop. "I'm not leaving again," he informed her. "I came back to say what I've said and to take care of you while you're sick, and that's what I'm going to do no matter what. But I can wait downstairs while you get dressed if you want. Maybe fix you something for breakfast?"

"Crackers are all I can eat in the morning. But if you're hungry, then you could have something—coffee or whatever you find in the kitchen—and I'll be there in a minute."

"Okay," he agreed, but he didn't go anywhere, he just kept standing there, watching her as if he thought she might sneak out on him if he didn't.

So Livi turned and went into her closet, closing the door between them.

She was genuinely cold now, so she dropped the towel

and dressed in a hurry, opting for the comfort of gray sweatpants and a white T-shirt that fitted like a ballet top.

Still chilled, she also pulled on a black angora shrug, then grabbed fuzzy socks and sat on the upholstered bench to pull them on.

But the minute she was sitting she forgot about putting on the socks. Because she was facing Patrick's side of the closet.

His clothes were all gone, but in her mind's eye she still saw his shirts and jackets and slacks hanging just the way they used to be.

And as she stared at that empty space, she realized how distant Patrick felt now. She'd had not thought of him whatsoever in all the time she'd spent getting ready for the previous evening's auction, spending that evening—and then the night—with Callan. She realized that even this morning Patrick had been only a reference point, that his memory hadn't had the kind of presence it had had for her since his death.

Instead, everything had been Callan, Callan, Callan...

Callan, who was not Patrick.

But who, it seemed, loved her and wanted her.

That wasn't something she'd ever expected to hear again. And now that she had, she had to admit that the words had meant every bit as much coming from Callan as they had when Patrick had said them.

Maybe it was time that it was Callan alone she thought about...

"I'm sorry, Patrick," she said. "But I...think it's time for me to move on." Because it was Callan's baby she was having. Callan waiting for her downstairs. Callan, who had just told her he loved her.

And who she had to admit she loved, too.

Callan, who was warm and kind and sweet and caring and compassionate—even if that wasn't always visible on the surface, it slipped out from behind a protective barrier when he let down his guard.

But Livi understood that. Not only because her own shyness sometimes made her the same way, but because of how Callan had grown up. Of course he would have to feel comfortable with people before he let himself be vulnerable with them. And of course he wouldn't be family oriented; of course being in close relationships was difficult for him.

But look what he made of himself, Livi thought.

Yes, maybe he'd caused a little trouble as a kid, but he'd grown up to be an enormous success. And with that success, he'd chosen to give back with his charity auction, to provide generously for the Tellers and Greta, bringing them into his home and life.

It didn't matter that it wasn't coming easy to him. It mattered that he was willing to do it. That he was working hard now on those relationships.

That he had the kind of character all those things spoke of.

So while Callan thought he couldn't *measure up* to Patrick, the more Livi thought about him, the more she knew he genuinely did.

Patrick had taken her out of her shell when she was a little girl, and Callan had brought her out of the grieving haze that she'd been denying she was in.

Callan had lured her out of the limbo she'd been left in since Patrick's death, and helped her to see that she *was* still alive and well and kicking—what he'd said the night she'd told him about Patrick.

Being with Callan opened her up. It made her see the

world again as a brighter, more hopeful place. It gave her a dimension outside the cocoon of her own family that she'd crawled into, and put her in a place where she saw a future for herself that she hadn't seen since Patrick's death. Callan had shown her that there honestly could be a full life for her again. And he'd given her a baby to help that along.

A baby she believed—now that she'd seen how Callan had prioritized his relationships with Greta and the Tellers—he wouldn't neglect. A baby who instead would benefit from the work Callan was doing to be a dad to Greta.

And most of all, he'd shown her that she was capable of loving another man—him. That even though she'd loved Patrick with all her heart and soul, he wasn't the *only* man she could love.

"Oh, Patrick, it isn't that I don't love you, too. I do. It's just that..."

It was just that she loved Callan equally as much.

Somehow she didn't feel as guilty for that as she'd thought she would. Instead she felt something else—a sort of peace in it, a strong sense that loving Callan, too, was okay, almost as if Patrick was there with her and letting her know that.

Maybe he was. Or maybe it was just that she'd known Patrick so well that she knew he *would* be okay with this. That he would *want* her to be happy even without him.

"Callan is a good man, Patrick," she assured her late husband, as if he really was there with her. "And there's a baby..."

A baby and more life waiting for her that she knew now she needed to live.

Livi suffered a moment of sadness to think that Patrick hadn't had more life himself. But even in that sadness she didn't feel held back. She finally felt ready, willing and able to move on.

Still staring at Patrick's side of the closet, she kissed the air—the way she would have hurriedly kissed Patrick goodbye before leaving the house for work.

Then she left the closet, sat on the edge of the bed to put on the fuzzy socks and went downstairs.

Callan was in the kitchen, just turning from her counter with two slices of toast on a plate as Livi reached the doorway.

"Hi," he said tentatively when he spotted her. "I know you said you didn't want anything, but I was thinking maybe a little dry toast..."

Livi went the rest of the way into the kitchen, standing on the opposite side of the counter from him. "Actually, the nausea seems to be going away early this morning," she told him, only realizing then that it was true.

He offered her the plate, but it wasn't food she wanted. It was him. She just wasn't sure how to get their previous conversation back on track. So she took the plate and a bite of the toast to buy herself a moment.

"Coffee, too?" Callan asked.

She shook her head, set the plate on the counter between them and said, "I don't really want anything to eat or drink, but thanks for trying."

"Thanks for trying..." he repeated. "That isn't for more than the toast, is it? It isn't the start of a kiss-off?"

"It's only for the toast," she said, seeing that he was still fearing what she might say to him now that he'd opened up to her.

"I need to know something for sure," she said then.

"Anything."

"I need to know that what you said upstairs wasn't just what you thought you had to say. If you want a relationship with your child, then I'll support that completely. Our relationship doesn't have to be a part of it."

He shook his head. "I told you that I'd be here telling you that I love you even if there wasn't a baby on board."

"I know that's what you *said*, but…I'm not a teenage girl in trouble, Callan. I don't need to be made an honest woman. And we can raise a child together without being anything to each other."

He closed his eyes and took a breath, as if bracing himself. Then he opened them and said fatalistically, "You don't want anything with me. You won't even give me a chance—"

"No, that's not what I'm saying. You said you talked to John Sr. this morning, and if this is coming from him pressuring you to 'do the right thing'—"

"I didn't even tell him about the baby. All we talked about was how he feels about Maeve and Greta, and how it's nothing to him to have uprooted his whole life, because otherwise he wouldn't have Maeve. Or Greta. And I realized that I feel the same way about you."

"You'd uproot your life for me?" she joked.

"Yes," Callan said without hesitation.

"You're sure? You're already stretched pretty thin…" she said, persisting with the joke just to give him a hard time.

"I've never been more sure of anything in my life than that I want you. Sure enough to risk Mandy coming back to haunt me for bringing in a Camden to co-parent her daughter."

"So it *was* a proposal upstairs?" Livi asked, recalling that the exact words had not been spoken.

"What did you think it was?"

"Just making sure."

"Because you want to know what you're saying no to?" There was just enough cockiness in his tone to let her know he was feeling less vulnerable. But she liked that.

"I'm not saying no," she told him, going on to also tell him how wrong he was to think even for a minute that he didn't measure up to Patrick in her eyes, how great she thought he was.

"But I've had the real thing," she concluded. "And I don't want to go from that to someone being with me because there's a gun to his back."

Callan grinned and stepped around the counter. He took her arm and turned her to face him. "I was thinking that it might take a gun to *your* back to get you where I want you."

"You mean, as part of your family?" Livi said.

"Is that what we can all be?" he asked, testing the waters. "Is that what you'll let us be? Because I may be lousy at it, but it's what I want. With you. You and them and this baby."

"Families come in all shapes and sizes," she allowed.

"But will you—can you—come and be that with the rest of us?"

She knew what he was asking—if she could leave her past behind. If she would.

Livi didn't have to think any more about it before she told him what she'd realized while she was in the closet, even telling him that she believed they had Patrick's blessing.

"I don't know how it happened," she said. "I didn't

think it *could* happen. But I love you, Callan. Just as much as I loved Patrick."

Callan's eyebrows shot up as if that came as a surprise to him. "You're not just saying *that*, are you?"

"I'm not. I guess there really can be more than one love of my life."

"A two-and-only?" he said.

Livi laughed at the made-up phrase. "I don't think there is such a thing. Maybe we should just look at it as the second half for us both. And in this half, you'll be the one-and-only man I have a baby with, a family with..."

"Oh, I like that!" he said effusively, and if she wasn't mistaken, his eyes suddenly had a little extra moisture in them.

Then both his hands went to her arms, clamping them gently but firmly—as if to keep her from getting away. "So will you marry me, Livi?"

"I will," she said, surprised to ever be saying that again.

Callan smiled once more before he pulled her close enough to kiss her, so deeply that it laid bare all his feelings for her and chased away any last doubts.

When the kiss ended, he pressed her close, holding her head to his chest. "I don't know how this morning-sickness thing works. Is kissing a bad thing?"

She laughed again. "Not this morning."

But with her own arms around him, her hands grasping his strong back, and his arms wrapping her like a big, warm comforter, it all felt too good to disturb by raising her face even to have him kiss her again.

Instead she just stood there with him holding her, her holding him, and letting herself get used to the fact that this would be where she belonged from here on.

In the arms of a man who wasn't Patrick.

But who had given her her life back and now wanted to share it with her.

Epilogue

"Oh, Conor, finally!" Kinsey Madison said when she connected with her brother for a video chat.

It was six o'clock on Monday morning and she'd been waiting tensely for this since 5:00 a.m. to accommodate the time difference between Denver and Germany.

"Is Declan okay?" she asked.

"He came through the third surgery just fine," her oldest brother said. "He's in recovery. They were able to save the leg."

"Thank God," Kinsey said. "Is he awake?"

"Not completely or I'd let you talk to him—I'm in recovery with him. He's responsive, but he can only keep his eyes open for a few seconds before he drifts out again. That's normal. But what's important is that we'll have him back up and around before you know it."

"So he won't get a medical discharge," Kinsey concluded.

"He can apply for one, and at this point, get it if he wants it," Conor said.

"*If* he wants it. But you guys…" She shook her head in frustration. "You just won't ever do what I wish you would and come home for good."

"Actually," Conor said, as if he'd been waiting to surprise her, "I've filled out my discharge papers, Kins."

"Really?"

"Really. I haven't turned them in yet—and I won't right now, so I can stay with Declan until he's well again, to oversee his care. But after that…"

Kinsey sighed. "After that there will be some other reason for you not to turn in the papers, and the three of you still won't come home," she said dejectedly.

Raised by an ex-military stepfather, her brothers had had the military and service to country ingrained in them from earliest childhood.

"Things are different this time," Conor said, but not with enough conviction to convince her. "With the drawdown to reduce active-duty forces, the ranks are being trimmed. Could be I can do more stateside."

"In Denver?" Kinsey asked dubiously, knowing she shouldn't get her hopes up.

"I don't know, maybe. I know from here Declan will go to Bethesda, Maryland, and I'll go with him. Then we'll see. But once he's doing well in Maryland, I'll come home for a visit, anyway."

Visits were all that ever actually happened. Brief visits that were few and far, far between.

Without pinning too many hopes on anything, she said, "So I'll at least get to see you—and maybe Declan once he's on the mend. And how's Liam?"

"He's good. He made it to the base yesterday before

we left on transport. He's talking about the drawdown, too. Who knows, you might have all three of us back in the next year."

"I know what you guys are doing, Conor. You want to make me think there's that chance so I don't do anything about the Camdens."

"We know you're alone now that Mom's gone, Kins. None of us like that. We all feel bad about it—"

She cut him off to say, "I've met them—the Camdens—since I talked to you last…"

"Oh, no! You told them?" Conor moaned. "You said we could talk more about it before you would."

"I haven't *done* anything. I met them by happenstance. Remember the job I took with the Tellers? That I could start in Northbridge and then transition back to Denver? Well, it's a long story I won't go into now, but Livi Camden got involved with the Tellers' granddaughter, Greta, and I met Livi through that. Then I went to one of the Camden Sunday dinners and met the rest of them. I think it's a sign."

"It *isn't* a sign," Conor insisted. "It's a coincidence, Kinsey. And not a far-reaching one. We grew up in Northbridge and that's where the Camdens were from. You were there to take care of Mom, and then went to Denver, where the Camdens live. It's not like you went to the ends of the earth and bumped into one of them—*that* would be a sign."

"Mom told me the truth about our father so I could look up the Camdens. So I wouldn't be alone, since you guys keep going off halfway around the world," Kinsey said, taking a different tack.

"Mom told you to explain where all that money came from," Conor corrected. "Mom and Hugh Madison were our parents. They're who raised us. Our biological father doesn't matter. Just have some patience, Kinsey. I'm coming home. Declan may *need* to come home. And if we both do, maybe Liam will, too. Just let the other lay."

But Kinsey didn't know if she could do that.

Now that she knew she and her brothers were all half Camdens, she just wasn't sure she could keep it quiet.

* * * * *

Love the Camdens? Well, there are still some left to meet... Look for Kinsey and Sutter's story, coming in March 2017 only from Harlequin Special Edition.

Drake Carson is willing to put up with Luce Hale, the supposed "expert" his mother brought to the ranch, as long as she can get the herd of wild horses off his land, but the pretty academic wants to study them instead! Sparks are sure to fly when opposites collide in Mustang Creek...

Read on for a sneak peek from New York Times *bestselling author Linda Lael Miller's second book in* THE CARSONS OF MUSTANG CREEK *trilogy,* ALWAYS A COWBOY, *coming September 2016 from HQN Books.*

CHAPTER ONE

THE WEATHER JUST plain sucked, but that was okay with Drake Carson. In his opinion, rain was better than snow any day of the week, and as for sleet…well, that was wicked, especially in the wide-open spaces, coming at a person in stinging blasts like a barrage of buckshot. Yep, give him a slow, gentle rainfall every time, the kind that generally meant spring was in the works. Anyhow, he could stand to get a little wet. Here in Wyoming, this close to the mountains, the month of May might bring sunshine and pastures blanketed with wildflowers, but it could also mean a rogue snowstorm fit to bury folks and critters alike.

Raising his coat collar around his ears, he nudged his horse into motion with his heels. Starburst obeyed, although he seemed hesitant about it, even edgy, and Drake wondered why. For almost a year now, livestock had gone missing—mostly calves, but the occasional steer or heifer, too. While it didn't happen often, for a rancher, a single lost animal was one too many. The spread was big, and he couldn't keep an eye on the whole place at once, of course.

He sure as hell tried, though.

"Stay with me," he told his dogs, Harold and Violet, a pair of German shepherds from the same litter and some of the best friends he'd ever had.

Then, tightening the reins slightly, in case Starburst took a notion to bolt out of his easy trot, he looked around, narrowing his eyes to see through the downpour. Whatever he'd expected to spot—a grizzly or a wildcat or a band of modern-day rustlers, maybe—he *hadn't* expected a lone female just up ahead, crouched behind a small tree and clearly drenched, despite the dark rain slicker covering her slender form.

She was peering through a pair of binoculars, having taken no apparent notice of Drake, his dogs or his horse. Even with the rain pounding down, they should have been hard to miss, being only fifty yards away.

Whoever this woman might be, she wasn't a neighbor or a local, either. Drake would have recognized her if she'd lived in or around Mustang Creek, and the whole ranch was posted against trespassers, mainly to keep tourists out. A lot of visiting sightseers had seen a few too many G-rated animal movies and thought they could cozy up to a bear, a bison or a wolf for a selfie to post on social media.

Most times, if the damn fools managed to get away alive, they were missing a few body parts or the family pet.

Drake shook off the images and concentrated on the subject at hand—the woman in the rain slicker.

Who was she, and what was she doing on Carson property?

A stranger, yes.

But it dawned on Drake that, whatever else she might be, she *wasn't* the reason his big Appaloosa was suddenly so skittish.

The woman was fixated on the wide meadow, actually

a shallow valley, just beyond the copse of cottonwood, and so, Drake realized now, was Starburst.

He stood in his stirrups and squinted, and his heart picked up speed as he caught sight—finally—of the band of wild mustangs grazing there. Once numbering only half a dozen or so, the herd had grown to more than twenty.

Now, alerted by the stallion, their leader and the unqualified bane of Drake's existence, they scattered.

He was vigilant, that devil on four feet, and cocky, too.

He lingered for a few moments while the mares fled in the opposite direction, tossed his magnificent head and snorted.

Too late, sucker.

Drake cursed under his breath and promptly forgot all about the woman who shouldn't have been there in the first damn place, his mind on the expensive mare—make that *mares*—the stallion had stolen from him. He whistled through his teeth, the piercing whistle that brought tame horses running, ready for hay, a little sweet feed and a warm stall.

He hadn't managed to get this close to the stallion and his growing harem in a long while, and he hated to let the opportunity pass, but he knew that if he gave chase, the dogs would be right there with him, and probably wind up getting their heads kicked in.

The stallion whinnied, taunting him, and sped away, topping the rise on the other side of the meadow and vanishing with the rest.

The dogs whimpered, itching to run after them, but Drake ordered them to stay; then he whipped off his hat, rain be damned, and smacked it hard against his thigh in pure exasperation. This time, he cussed in earnest.

Harold and Violet were fast and they were agile, but he'd raised them from pups and he couldn't risk letting them get hurt.

Hope stirred briefly when Drake's prize chestnut quarter horse, a two-year-old mare destined for greatness, reappeared at the crest of the hill opposite, ears pricked at the familiar whistle, but the stallion came back for her, crowding her, nipping at her neck and flanks, and then she was gone again.

Damn it all to hell.

"Thanks for nothing, mister."

It was the intruder, the trespasser. The woman stormed toward Drake through the rain-bent grass, waving the binoculars like a maestro raising a baton at the symphony. If he hadn't been so annoyed by her mere presence, let alone her nerve—yelling at him like that when *she* was the one in the wrong—he might have been amused.

She was a sight for sure, plowing through the grass, all fuss and fury and wet to the skin.

Mildly curious now that the rush of adrenaline roused by losing another round to that son-of-a-bitching stallion was beginning to subside, Drake waited with what was, for him, uncommon patience. He hoped the approaching tornado, pint-size but definitely category five, wouldn't step on a snake before she completed the charge.

Born and raised on this land, he wouldn't have stomped around like that, not without keeping a close eye out for rattlers.

As she got closer, he made out an oval face, framed by the hood of her coat, and a pair of amber eyes that flashed as she demanded, "Do you have any idea how long it took me to get that close to those horses? Days!

And what happens? *You* have to come along and ruin everything!"

Drake resettled his hat, tugging hard at the brim, and waited.

The woman all but stamped her feet. "Days!" she repeated wildly.

Drake felt his mouth twitch. "Excuse me, ma'am, I'm a bit confused. You're here because...?"

"Because of the horses!" The tone and pitch of her voice said he was an idiot for even asking. Apparently he ought to be able to read her mind instead.

He gave himself points for politeness—and for managing a reasonable tone. "I see," he said, although of course he didn't.

"The least you could do is apologize," she informed him, glaring.

Still mounted, Drake adjusted his hat again. The dogs sat on either side of him and Starburst, staring at the woman as if she'd sprung up out of the ground.

When he replied, he sounded downright amiable. In his own opinion, anyway. "Apologize? Now, why would I do that? Given that I *live* here, I mean. This is private property, Ms.—"

She wasn't at all fazed to find out that she was on somebody else's land, uninvited. Nor did she offer her name.

"It took me hours to track those horses down," she ranted on, still acting like the offended party, "in this weather, no less! I finally get close enough, and you... you..." She paused, but only to suck in a breath so she could go right on strafing him with words. "*You* try hiding behind a tree without moving a muscle, waiting practically forever and with water dripping down your neck."

He might have pointed out that he was no stranger to inclement weather, since he rode fence lines in blizzards and rounded up strays under a hot sun—and those were the *easy* days—but he refrained. "What were you doing there, behind my tree?"

"*Your* tree? No one owns a tree."

"Maybe not, but people can own the ground it grows on. And that's the case here, I'm afraid."

She rolled her eyes.

Great, a tree hugger. She probably drove one of those little hybrid cars, plastered with bumper stickers, and cruised along at thirty miles an hour in the left lane.

Nobody loved nature more than he did, but hell, the Carsons had held the deed to this ranch for more than a century, and it wasn't a public campground with hiking trails, nor was it a state park.

Drake leaned forward in the saddle. "Do the words *no trespassing* mean anything to you?" he asked sternly.

On some level, though, he was enjoying this encounter way more than he should have.

She merely glowered up at him, arms folded, chin raised.

He sighed. "All right. Let's see if we can clarify matters. That tree—" he gestured to the one she'd taken refuge behind earlier, and spoke very slowly so she'd catch his drift "—is on land my family owns. I'm Drake Carson. And you are?"

The look of surprise on her face was gratifying. "*You're* Drake Carson?"

"I was when I woke up this morning," he said in a deliberate drawl. "I don't imagine that's changed since then." A measured pause. "Now, how about answering my original question? What are you doing here?"

She seemed to wilt, and Drake supposed that was a victory, however small, but he wasn't inclined to celebrate. "I'm studying the horses."

The brim of his hat spilled water down his front as he nodded. "Well, yeah, I kind of figured that. It's really not the point, now, is it? Like I said, this is private property. And if you'd asked permission to be here, I'd know it."

She blushed, but no explanation was forthcoming. "So you're *him*."

"Yes, ma'am. You—"

The next moment, she was blustering again. "Tall man on a tall horse," she remarked, her tone scathing.

A few seconds earlier, he'd been in charge here. Now he felt defensive, which was ridiculous.

He drew a deep breath, released it slowly and spoke with quiet authority. He hoped. "My height and my horse have nothing to do with anything, as far as I can see. My point, once again, is you don't have the right to be here, much less yell at me."

"Yes, I do."

Of all the freaking gall. Drake glowered at the young woman standing next to his horse by then, unafraid, giving as good as she got. "What?"

"I *do* have the right to be here," she insisted. "I asked your mother's permission to come out and study the wild horses, and she said yes. In fact, she was very supportive."

Well, shit.

Would've been nice if his mother had bothered to mention it to him.

For some reason, he couldn't back off, or not completely, anyway. Call it male pride. "Okay," he said evenly. "*Why* do you want to study wild horses? Considering that they're…*wild* and everything."

She seemed thoroughly undaunted. "I'm doing my graduate thesis on how wild horses exist and interact with domesticated animals on working ranches." She added with emphasis, "And how ranchers deal with them. Like you."

So he was part of the equation. Yippee.

"Just so you understand," he said, "you aren't going to study *me*."

"What if I got your mother's permission?" she asked sweetly.

"Very funny." By then, Drake's mood was headed straight downhill. What was he doing out here in the damn rain, bantering with some self-proclaimed intellectual, when all he'd had before leaving the house this morning was a skimpy breakfast and one cup of coffee? The saddle leather creaked as he bent toward her. "Listen, Ms. Whoever-you-are, I don't give a rat's ass about your thesis, or your theories about ranchers and wild horses, either. Do what you have to do, try not to get yourself killed and then move on to whatever's next on your agenda—preferably elsewhere."

Not surprisingly, the woman wasn't intimidated. "Hale," she announced brightly. "My name is Lucinda Hale, but everybody calls me Luce."

He inhaled, a long, deep breath. If he'd ever had that much trouble learning a woman's name before, he didn't recall the occasion. "Ms. Hale, then," he began, tugging at the brim of his hat in a gesture that was more automatic than cordial. "I'll leave you to it. While I'm sure your work is absolutely fascinating, I have plenty of my own to do. In short, while I've enjoyed shadowboxing with you, I'm fresh out of leisure time."

He might've been talking to a wall. "Oh, don't worry,"

she said cheerfully. "I wouldn't *dream* of interfering. I'll be an observer, that's all. Watching, figuring out how things work, making a few notes. You won't even know I'm around."

Drake sighed inwardly and reined his horse away, although he didn't use his heels. The dogs, still fascinated by the whole scenario, sat tight. "You're right, Ms. Hale. I won't know you're around, because you won't be. Around *me*, that is."

"You really are a very difficult man," she observed almost sadly. "Surely you can see the value of my project. Interactions between wild animals, domesticated ones and human beings?"

LUCE WAS COLD, wet, a little amused and *very* intrigued.

Drake Carson was gawking at her as though she'd just popped in from a neighboring dimension, wearing a tutu and waving a wand. His two beautiful dogs, waiting obediently for some signal from their master, seemed equally curious.

The consternation on his face was absolutely priceless.

And a very handsome face it was, at least what she could see of it in the shadow of his hat brim. If he had the same features as his younger brother, Mace, whom she'd met earlier that day, he was one very good-looking man.

She decided to push him a bit further. "You run this ranch, don't you?"

"I do my best."

She liked his voice, which was calm and carried a low drawl. "Then you're the one I want."

Oh, no, she thought, that came out all wrong.

"For my project, I mean."

His strong jawline tightened visibly. "I don't have time

to babysit you," he said. "This is a working ranch, not a resort."

"As I've said repeatedly, Mr. Carson, you won't have to do anything of the sort. I can take care of myself, and I'll stay out of your way as much as possible."

He seemed unconvinced. Even irritated.

But he didn't ride away.

Luce had already been warned that he wouldn't take to her project.

Talk about an understatement.

Mentally, she cataloged the things she'd learned about Drake Carson.

He was in charge of the ranch, which spanned thousands of acres and was home to lots of cattle and horses, as well as wildlife. The Carsons had very deep ties to Bliss County, Wyoming, going back several generations. He loved the outdoors, was good with animals, especially horses.

He was, in fact, a true cowboy.

He was also on the quiet side, solitary by nature, slow to anger—but watch out if he did. At thirty-two, Drake had never been married; he was college-educated, and once he'd gotten his degree, he'd come straight back to the ranch, having no desire to live anywhere else. He worked from sunrise to sunset and often longer.

Harry, the housekeeper whose real name was Harriet Armstrong, had dished up some sort of heavenly pie when Luce had arrived at the main ranch house, fairly early in the day. As soon as she understood who Luce was and why she was there, she'd proceeded to spill information about Drake at a steady clip.

Luce had encountered Mace Carson, Drake's younger brother, very briefly, when he'd come in from the family vineyard expressly for a piece of pie. Harry had introduced them and explained Luce's mission—i.e., to gather material for her thesis and interview Drake in depth, and get the rancher's perspective.

Mace had smiled slightly and had shaken his head in response. "I'm glad you're here, Ms. Hale, but I'm afraid my brother isn't going to be a whole lot of use as a research subject. He's into his work and not much else, and he doesn't like to be distracted from it. Makes him testy."

A quick glance in Harry's direction had confirmed the sinking sensation created by Mace's words. The other woman had given a small, reluctant nod of agreement.

Well, Luce thought now, standing face-to-horse with Drake, they'd certainly known what they were talking about.

Drake was *definitely* testy.

He stared grimly into the rainy distance for a long moment, then muttered, "As if that damn stallion wasn't enough to get under my skin—"

"Cheer up," Luce said. She loved a challenge. "I'm here to help."

Drake gave her a long, level look. "Why didn't you say so in the first place?" he drawled, without a hint of humor. He flung out his free hand for emphasis, the reins resting easily in the other one. "My problems are over."

"Didn't you tell me you were leaving?" Luce asked.

He opened his mouth, closed it again, evidently reconsidering whatever he'd been about to say. Finally, with a mildly defensive note in his voice, he went on. "I planned to," he said, "but if I did, you'd be out here alone." He looked around. "Where's your horse? You won't be getting close to those critters again today. The stallion will see to that."

Luce's interest was genuine. "You sound as if you know him pretty well."

"We understand each other, all right," Drake said. "We should. We've been playing this game for a couple of years now."

That tidbit was going in her notes.

She shook her head in belated answer to his question about her means of transportation. "I don't have a horse," she explained. "I parked on a side road and hiked out here."

The day had been breathtakingly beautiful, before the clouds lowered and thickened and dumped rain. She'd hiked in all the western states and in Europe, and this was some gorgeous country. The Grand Tetons were just that. Grand.

"The nearest road is miles from here. You came all this way *on foot*?" Drake frowned at her. "Did my mother know you were crazy when she agreed to let you do your study here?"

"I actually enjoy hiking. A little rain doesn't bother me. I'll dry off back at the ranch."

"Back at the ranch?" he repeated slowly. Warily.

This was where she could tell him that his mother and hers were old friends, but she chose not to do it. She didn't want to take advantage of that relationship—or at least *appear* to be taking advantage of it. "That's a beautiful house you live in, by the way. Not what I expected to find on a place like this—chandeliers and oil paintings and wainscoting and all. Hardly the Ponderosa." She beamed a smile at Drake. "I was planning to camp out, but your mother generously invited me to stay on the ranch. My room has a wonderful view of the mountains. It's going to be glorious, waking up to that every morning."

Drake, she soon discovered, was still a few beats behind. "You're *staying* with us?"

"How else can I observe you in your native habitat?" Luce offered up another smile, her most innocent one. The truth was, she intended to camp some of the time, if only to avoid the long walk from the house. One of the main reasons she'd chosen this specific project was Drake himself, although she certainly wasn't going to tell him that! She'd known, even before Harry filled her in on the more personal aspects of his life, that he was an animal advocate, as well as a prominent rancher, that he had a degree in ecology. She'd first seen his name in print when she was still an undergrad, just a quote in an article, expressing his belief that running a large cattle operation could be done without endangering wildlife or the environment. Knowing that her mother and Blythe Carson were close had been a deciding factor, too, of course—a way of gaining access.

She allowed herself a few minutes to study the man. He sat on his horse confidently relaxed and comfortable in the saddle, the reins loosely held. The well-trained animal stood there calmly, clipping grass but not moving otherwise during their discussion.

Drake broke into her reverie by saying, "Guess I'd better take you back before something happens to you." He leaned toward her, reaching down. "Climb on."

She looked at the proffered hand and bit her lip, hesitant to explain that she'd ridden only once—an ancient horse at summer camp when she was twelve, and she'd been terrified the whole time.

No, she couldn't tell him that. Her pride wouldn't let her.

Besides, she wouldn't be steering the huge gelding; Drake would. And there was no denying the difficulties the weather presented.

She'd gotten some great footage during the afternoon and made a few notes, which meant the day wasn't a total loss.

"My backpack's heavy," she pointed out, her brief courage faltering. The top of that horse was pretty far off the ground. She could climb mountains, for Pete's sake, but that was different; she'd been standing on her own two feet the whole time.

At last, Drake smiled, and the impact of that smile was palpable. He was still leaning toward her, still holding out his hand. "Starburst's knees won't buckle under the weight of a backpack," he told her. "Or your weight, either."

The logic was irrefutable.

Drake slipped his booted foot out from the stirrup to make room for hers. "Come on. I'll haul you up behind me."

She handed up the backpack, sighed heavily. "Okay," she said. Then, gamely, she took Drake's hand. His grip was strong, and he swung her up behind him with no apparent effort.

It was easy to imagine this man working with horses and digging postholes for fences.

Settled on the animal's broad back, Luce had no choice but to put her arms around his lean waist and hang on. For dear life.

The rain was coming down harder, and conversation was impossible.

Gradually, Luce relaxed enough to loosen her grip on Drake's middle.

A little, anyway.

Now that she was fairly sure she wasn't facing certain death, Luce allowed herself to enjoy the ride. Intrepid hiker though she was, the thought of trudging back to her car in a driving rain made her wince.

She hadn't missed the irony of the situation, either. She wanted to study wild horses, but she didn't know how to ride a tame one. Drake would be well within his rights to point that out to her, although she sensed, somehow, that he wouldn't.

When they finally reached the ranch house, he was considerate enough not to laugh when she slid clumsily off the horse and almost landed on her rear in a giant puddle. No, he simply tugged at the brim of his hat, suppressing a smile, and rode away without looking back.

Don't miss
ALWAYS A COWBOY
by New York Times *bestselling author*
Linda Lael Miller,
available wherever HQN books and
ebooks are sold.

COMING NEXT MONTH FROM

(H) HARLEQUIN®

SPECIAL EDITION

Available September 20, 2016

#2503 MS. BRAVO AND THE BOSS
The Bravos of Justice Creek • by Christine Rimmer
Jed Walsh has finally found the perfect assistant to put up with his extreme writing process in a down-on-her-luck caterer named Elise Bravo. He refuses to give in to their attraction and vows to make her stay on as his assistant, but he never thought she'd be able to lay claim to the heart he didn't even know he had.

#2504 MAVERICK VS. MAVERICK
Montana Mavericks: The Baby Bonanza • by Shirley Jump
Lindsay Dalton is drawn to Walker Jones III from the first time she sees him. The only problem? Their first meeting is in a courthouse—and she's suing him! Walker has met his match in Lindsay, but when they are forced to work together, they might just have more in common than they ever expected.

#2505 ROPING IN THE COWGIRL
Rocking Chair Rodeo • by Judy Duarte
Shannon Cramer is a nurse at the Rocking Chair Rodeo, a retirement home for cowboys. When she and Blake Darnell, a headstrong attorney, butt heads over a May-December romance between his uncle and her aunt, they're surprised to encounter sparks of desire and a romance of their own.

#2506 BUILDING THE PERFECT DADDY
Those Engaging Garretts! • by Brenda Harlen
Lauryn Garrett has no intention of falling for the sexy handyman in charge of her home renovations, but Ryder Wallace knows how to fix all kinds of things—even a single mother's broken heart. As eager as Ryder is to get his hands on Lauryn's house, it is the wounded woman who lives there who can teach him a thing or two about building a family.

#2507 THE MAN SHE SHOULD HAVE MARRIED
The Crandall Lake Chronicles • by Patricia Kay
Olivia Britton may be developing feelings for Matt Britton, her dead husband's brother, but his mother is trying to have her declared an unfit mother to little Thea, the daughter her husband never got to meet. Matt's been in love with Olivia for years and he's not going to let his mother's prejudice get in their way. Can they overcome a bitter mother-in-law and a lawsuit to create the family they've always dreamed of?

#2508 A WEDDING WORTH WAITING FOR
Proposals in Paradise • by Katie Meyer
Samantha Farley is back in Paradise, Florida, once again trying to fit in and make friends, now with the added pressure of her job riding on the outcome. Dylan Turner offers to use his status as town heartthrob to boost her social profile, secretly hoping to convince her they'd be perfect together. Will they be able to handle town gossip and past heartbreaks to find their way to happily-ever-after?

YOU CAN FIND MORE INFORMATION ON UPCOMING HARLEQUIN® TITLES, FREE EXCERPTS AND MORE AT WWW.HARLEQUIN.COM.

HSECNM0916

SPECIAL EXCERPT FROM

H HARLEQUIN®

SPECIAL EDITION

*Walker Jones III and Lindsay Dalton go head-to-head
in a lawsuit, but their legal maneuvering could lead to
an epic romantic showdown outside the courtroom!*

*Read on for a sneak preview of
MAVERICK VS. MAVERICK
by Shirley Jump, the next book in the
MONTANA MAVERICKS: THE BABY BONANZA
continuity.*

"Dance with me."

Her eyes widened. "Dance…with you?"

"Come on." He swayed his hips and swung their arms. She stayed stiff, reluctant. He could hardly blame her. After all, just a few hours ago, they'd been facing off in court. "It's the weekend. Let's forget about court cases and arguments and just…"

"Have fun?" She arched a brow.

He shot her a grin. "I hear they do that, even in towns as small as Rust Creek Falls."

That made her laugh. Her hips were swaying along with his, though she didn't seem to be aware she was moving to the beat. "Are you saying my town is boring?"

Boring? She had no idea. But he wouldn't tell her that. Instead he gave her his patented killer smile. "I'm saying it's a small town. With some great music on the juke and a dance floor just waiting for you." He lifted her hand and spun her to the right, then back out again to the left.

"Come on, Ms. Dalton, dance with me. Me the man, not me the corporation you're suing."

She hesitated, and he could see his opportunity slipping away. Why did it matter that this woman—of all the women in this room, including the quartet flirting with him—dance with him?

"I shouldn't…" She started to slide her hand out of his.

He stepped closer to her. "Shouldn't have fun? Shouldn't dance with the enemy?"

"I shouldn't do anything with the enemy."

He grinned. "I'm not asking for anything. Just a dance."

Another song came on the juke, and the blonde and her friends started up again, moving from one side of the dance floor to the other. Their movements swept Walker and Lindsay into the middle of the dance floor, leaving her with two choices—dance with him or wade through the other women to escape.

For a second, he thought he'd won and she was going to dance with him. Then the smile on her face died, and she shook her head. "I'm sorry, Mr. Jones, but I don't dance with people who don't take responsibility for their mistakes."

Then she turned on her heel and left the dance floor and, a moment later, the bar.

EXCLUSIVE
Limited Time Offer

$1.⁰⁰ OFF

New York Times bestselling author

LINDA LAEL MILLER

introduces you to the middle of the three Carson brothers.

He's as stubborn as they come—and he won't thank a beautiful stranger for getting in his way!

Always a Cowboy

Available August 30, 2016.
Pick up your copy today!

HQN™

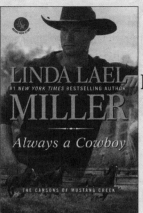

$7.99 U.S./$9.99 CAN.

$1.⁰⁰ OFF   the purchase price of ALWAYS A COWBOY by Linda Lael Miller.

Offer valid from August 30, 2016, to September 30, 2016.
Redeemable at participating retail outlets. Not redeemable at Barnes & Noble.
Limit one coupon per purchase. Valid in the U.S.A. and Canada only.